This volume of short stories brings together different voices that speak of the vagaries of human experience, of vignettes of human emotions that resonate so much in the times we live too. Translated in a wonderfully lucid style, these stories by great writers from the Indian subcontinent, known and little known, in the genre will surely have a worldwide appeal.

– **Dr. Nishi Pulugurtha, Academic and Author**

Chaitali Sengupta brings together in translation a dozen short stories written by a galaxy of writers of the Indian subcontinent. Sengupta admirably captures the energy, texture, and voice of an interesting mix of stories of diverse shades, each author displaying a distinctive style. In her sensitive engagement with the source texts, she is unambiguous and transparent and this makes the volume eminently readable.

- **Amita Ray, Academic, author, translator**

The art of translation is intricate, for the essence of the story must be retained. I must congratulate Chaitali Sengupta for her effort in sharing the impressive stories of Bengali and Hindi authors, by beautifully translating them into English. The translation is marvellously accurate. She has selected the most appealing stories, the simple nature lover: Bolai, or the salt inspector who is in a dilemma to choose between ethics and money, the pathos of poverty in 'A winter's night'. It takes courage to translate the Nobel Laureate Tagore, the learned Jai Shankar Prasad and the detailed presentation of the evergreen author Premchand, and Sengupta has done this with great elan and has acquainted us with many memorable stories. Through her work, Sengupta has given us an insight into the Indian mindset, in which the global English reader can identify glimpses of himself/herself.

- **Ipsita Sharan, Academic reviewer**

Timeless Tales in Translation

Timeless Tales in Translation

A Representative Anthology of Bengali and Hindi Short Stories

Translated by
Chaitali Sengupta

BLACK EAGLE BOOKS
DUBLIN, USA | BBSR, INDIA

Black Eagle Books
USA address:
7464 Wisdom Lane
Dublin, OH 43016

India address:
E/312, Trident Galaxy, Kalinga Nagar,
Bhubaneswar-751003, Odisha, India

E-mail: info@blackeaglebooks.org
Website: www.blackeaglebooks.org

First International Edition Published by
Black Eagle Books, 2022

TIMELESS TALES IN TRANSLATION
by **Bengali & Hindi Eminent Writers**
Translated by **Chaitali Sengupta**

Translation Copyright © **Chaitali Sengupta**
Illustration copyright © **Sumitra Roy**

Cover & Interior Design: Ezy's Publication

ISBN- 978-1-64560-328-3 (Paperback)
Library of Congress Control Number: 2022919976

Printed in the United States of America

Dedication

In the loving memory of **Lopamudra Sarkar**
who left us too soon

Foreword

Translated literature facilitates making familiar the diverse world of races, religions and cultures, the other no longer remains alien. Literary translations construct bridges of cultural understanding, the unknown shrouded in mystery and the mists of ignorance becomes familiar, comprehensible and brings the people of the world closer, emphatically reiterating that universal humanism lies at the core of a literary text, irrespective of its medium of expression.

Some incorrigible experts may sometimes rue the losses incurred in literary translation, due to the inadequacies of corresponding words in the source language. But literary translation is not about semantic jugglery, literary translation is not just about translating words, it is about translating the unknown in definable terms; it is about creating an intimacy between the home and the world. Literary translation is an enabling familiarizing process that deconstructs the traditional pride and prejudices about the unknown, unfamiliar Other. It liberates one from the myopia of national boundaries and creates international cultural understanding, though the context may be rooted in Bengal, Boston or Brazil.

Translator Chaitali Sengupta states that the *Timeless Tales in Translations* is her third book of translations. In her note as translator, she explains in detail that her choice of the twelve short stories written by eight celebrated authors of colonial India has been an informed choice. The span of the period represented is about 100 years, from 1855 to 1955. First of all, credit is due to the translator as she has competently translated into English, stories written in three Indian languages, Bengali, Hindi and Urdu. This is not a common skill.

Interestingly, seven of the selected authors whose short stories Sengupta has translated are male authors. The only female writer to be included is Swarnakumari Devi, elder sister of litterateur Rabindranath Tagore, who received the Nobel Prize in 1913. This positioning of Swarnakumari Devi as the first writer in this anthology is a game changer of sorts. Usually, Tagore is recognized as the pioneering figure of the Indian short story. However, by placing two of Swarnakumari's stories as the first stories that demand our attention for their timelessness, Sengupta has turned the floodlights towards the first woman writer of fiction in Bengal. Though there are claims made by a few others, but most literary critics of Bengali literature agree that Swarnakumari Devi is indeed the first Bengali woman fictionist.

Interestingly, Sengupta has followed a chronological time-frame and so she has placed Rabindranath, five years junior to Swarnakumari, as the second of the timeless creators. Two stories of Rabindranath are followed by translations of stories by Saratchandra Chatterjee, Munshi Premchand, Rajshekhar Basu, Jaishankar Prasad, Bibhuti Bhusan Bandopadhyay and Saadat Hasan Manto, respectively. All the stories selected foreground certain timeless, universal emotions, feelings, sentiments, love, affection, conflict, pride, prejudice, social evils, empathy and transcendence. While Swarnakumari's story *"Why"* is an essentialist gendered narrative, her story on Bhim Singha proves that the writer can traverse wider expanses as the location of the story is centred in Rajasthan and focuses on valour, pride and dutifulness. Rabindranath's stories *"Bolai"* and *"Shubha"* are deeply emotive and strikingly varied in their themes, while Saratchandra Chatterjee's story about Ramlal expresses a compelling sense of turning humane and empathetic.

The short stories by Premchand and Jaishankar Prasad describe a different social environment and an entirely distinct geographical location in India. Premchand's stories about the Salt Inspector and the emotional attachment to the dog Jabra in *"A Winter's Night"* are outstanding tales of human values that transcend all barriers of social prejudices.

The stories of Rajshekhar Basu and Bibhuti Bhushan Bandopadhyay are atypical and create shock, surprise and wonder. While Rajshekhar Basu's story combines wit, humour and irony with great deftness, Bibhuti Bhushan's story *"The Atheist"* is a philosophic narrative that contrasts the rational and logical with the mystical and spiritual that is enshrined in the natural environment. The final story in this riveting collection of excellent short stories is Sadaat Hasan Manto's story *"Ten Rupees"* about sexual exploitation of poor minor girls is disturbing and nuanced at the same time.

Despite the problems that are embedded within translation practices, it is translation as cultural transfer that sensitizes the world about cultural diversity. The awareness about the specificities of location, race, religion, cultural practices, gender, sexuality and ethnicity can be built through the medium of translated texts. The babel of unfamiliar tongues generating incomprehensible cacophony can be decoded, deconstructed and re-created in the translated target language that will lead to cultural understanding and a sense of universal humanism.

I am certain that Chaitali Sengupta's book *Timeless Tales in Translation* will enchant, enrich and enlighten both global and local readers of Indian short stories.

Dr. Sanjukta Dasgupta
Convenor, English Advisory Board, Sahitya Akademi, New Delhi
President, Executive Committee, Intercultural Poetry and
Performance Library at ICCR, Kolkata
Visiting Professor, Jagiellonian University, Krakow, Poland (2018)
Professor, Dept of English (Retd), Former Dean, Faculty of Arts,
Calcutta University

Translator's note

In a country that has several regional languages, translation is the only way to prevent the regional languages from becoming obscure. Thankfully, the translation from Indian regional languages into English is, and has been for many years, steadily taking place. Had it not been for translation, many Indian authors would have remained unknown outside the Indian shores.

"Timeless tales in Translation" is my third translation work and comprises 12 short stories by famous Indian authors like Rabindranath Tagore, Swarnakumari Debi, Sarat Chandra Chatterjee, Munshi Premchand, Jaishankar Prasad, Rajsekhar Basu, Bibhuti Bhushan Bandopadhyay, Sadaat Hasan Manto. It represents the classic tales of writers in the vernacular languages of India- Bengali, Hindi, and Urdu. Chronologically, the earliest writer featuring in this collection is Swarnakumari Debi (1855-1932) and the latest author is Sadaat Hasan Manto (1912-1955). Since all their works are now available in the public domain, I did not have to get the copyright permission for these 12 stories.

Why have I chosen to translate the literary masterpieces of these above authors? The writers belong to the late nineteenth to mid-twentieth century. I was acquainted with their works in my college and university days. We all know how in the early decades of the twentieth century, Rabindranath Tagore strode like a colossus on the Indian literary scene. After he was awarded the Nobel prize in 1913, till date, his works have been translated into not only regional Indian languages but also into major European languages. Tagore is a vastly celebrated and translated author. But there are many other notable Indian authors, writing in other Indian languages. Their powerful, dazzling works still today have remained little known to the Western readers.

It is this thought that prompted me to translate their works. Besides, living away from India, I have also observed the curiosity of the non-Indians about Indian literature. I must confess that the desire to exchange the great linguistic diversity present in our vernacular literature also motivated me enough to carry forward this arduous task of translation.

Some stories that I have translated here are already translated before. But I sincerely believe that fresh translations of already translated works are also needed. The stories from both Hindi and Bengali literature are powerful representation of 'Indianness'- be it Jaishankar Prasad's *'In Charity'*, or Sarat Chandra Chatterjee's *'Ramlal's transformation'*. Premchand's *'A winter's night'* depicts the life and struggles of the farmers in colonial India. And although massive changes have come into their lives in these past seventy-five years, Premchand's world is still very much present in rural India. Through my translations, I wish to bring the English-speaking readers, both at home and abroad, to these authors and their times. My attempt is to connect India with the rest of the world, by enabling the foreign readers to glimpse the unfamiliar worlds of our stellar Indian writers.

There is, of course, another very important reason that nudged me to embark on this project. A great number of Indian young readers do not read in their mother tongue anymore. Slowly, but surely, a class of Indians is emerging who can speak an Indian language, but cannot read it well. I strongly believe that this group must be given Indian tales, epics, and literature in English translation. Translation, in this case, must act like a bridge between the literature of the past and present times. These works also need to be made available to them via their school, college, and university libraries and through their academic syllabi.

Translation is a challenging craft for many reasons. It is not only about translating a text in a different language, but it is more about retaining an emotion, delicate sensibilities, and culture, in the other language. A translator works to remove the linguistic barriers and attempts to recreate the same experience that the readers of the source language has. As a translator, I've tried to catch the spirit of the original, and convey it through the means of my translation. I have followed the original texts sincerely and have done my best to take all the qualities of the original work and yet find my own 'voice' running parallel to the original.

Lastly, I'm deeply indebted to Dr. Sanjukta Dasgupta, for her encouraging Foreword. She has been instrumental in putting my fears to rest about the quality of my translations. Her assurance enabled me to engage with the task of translation with more confidence. I am also indebted to Ms. Amita Roy's unfailing good judgement and perception of my other translation works. I am grateful to both of them for their scrutiny and encouragement. I extend my sincere thanks to Dr. Nishi Pulugurtha and Ms. Ipsita Sharan for their precious time and the wonderful blurb they wrote for this work of mine. My thanks to the publisher Mr. Satya Pattanaik (Black Eagle Books) for his immense help and enthusiasm in bringing out the first international edition. Lastly, I must thank Dr. Santosh Bakaya and Shri Gopal Lahiri, who gave valuable input during the initial stages of this task. I hope I have been able to put their feedback and trust to good use in this book.

Chaitali Sengupta

CONTENTS

Swarnakumari Devi

Prince Bhimsingha
Kumar Bhimsingha

The king of *Mewar* (A region in the south-central part of Rajasthan), Rana Raj Singha, was resting alone in his sleeping chamber. Dusk had set in. As per the orders of the king, the servants had kept only one lamp burning, extinguishing away the rest. The soft light had brought such an unctuous ambience to the spacious room that the king's thoughts, too, had taken a pleasing hue. The day of the coronation was almost upon them, the day when prince Jayasingha would be anointed his heir, the next king of Mewar. Rana Raj Singha's mind was full only with the thoughts of how elated his royal queen would be, on that special day, how happy the prince would indeed be. His mind was not concerned with how his subjects would react to this extraordinary event.

Suddenly, the gates of his royal chamber opened up, and his second queen, Kamal Kumari, entered. Startled, the king sat up on his bed, surprised to find her there. He indicated her to take a seat nearby. And when she took her seat near him, the king asked, "You, at this late hour?"

The queen replied, "There's no option left for me. You never show up when I ask for you."

Embarrassed, the king remembered that throughout the day, a couple of messages came from the queen, requesting him to visit her in the inner chambers of the palace. Slowly, he said, "My dear queen, I forgot."

Kamal Kumari's mind hissed. *Yes indeed, such is my fate that you've always forgotten me. There's nothing new about it.* Keeping her face expressionless, she only asked, "I just came to confirm; are the rumors that are brewing, true, my King?"

Something forced the king not to come out with a direct reply. He asked, "Which rumors do you mean?"

The Queen responded: "Rumours, that says that your throne is going to be taken over by Jayasingha, during your kingship. Looks like our land is following the Muslim rulers in this matter."

This sneering remark, aimed at Jaysingha, was not lost upon the king; he said, "Rumours are gossip. Not the truth. My throne is not being usurped by Jayasingha; on the contrary, I'm bestowing it upon him."

The queen laughed harshly. "Ah, so you're passing the throne to him. Why such a haste to abdicate, and take retirement, may I ask?"

Holding his surging anger in check, the king replied, "My dear queen, there's no reason to laugh like that. A king must think a hundred times and act with deep consideration. Just think, the well-being and suffering of his subjects are so much dependent on his decisions. If I, the reigning monarch, do not take a decision now, then chances are that in my absence, the question of succession would lead to a fight among the brothers, and ruin the kingdom."

The Queen said, "But my observation is, that in trying to find a solution, you're in fact, instigating one brother to fight the other. In the name of protecting your kingdom, you're leading it towards destruction. If you wish to decide on your successor, while you're still living, then pray, why do you not declare your eldest son as the next king? Why are you usurping his rightful eligibility to the throne unlawfully and relinquishing it to the younger one?"

The words rang true, but those did not please the king. Sometimes, it was difficult to bear the truth. With supreme irritation, the king said, "Bhimsingha and Jayasingha were both born almost at the same time. The problem is the difference in their time of birth is so minute, that based on that, Bhimsingha cannot claim to be the successor to the throne, just because he is elder by a few seconds. They're born on the same day, at the same time. Under the circumstance, the one who is more capable has a right to inherit the throne. I believe Jayasingha to be more capable of the two."

Laughing, the queen said, "It seems like you want to turn the wheel of time; or, else, why would you accept the younger one, to be equal to the eldest one? I'm happy that just your mere words would not change the dictates of time; even if a person is marginally older by birth, he deserves to be considered as the eldest. *Lav and Kush* (the children of Ram and Sita from the Hindu epic Ramayana) were twins; but then why did Lav succeed his father on the throne? Besides, let me ask you, on what grounds do you think Jayasingha is more deserving than Bhimsingha? Is Bhimsingha any less than Jayasingha in terms of bravery, honesty, intelligence, prowess? Whom do the army admire? Whose honesty enchants the nobles in your court? Whom do the subjects want as their future king? You'll get your answer, if only you ask others. However, if you believe Jayasingha to be more deserving, since he's born of your favourite consort, and is hence your dear prince, of course, that is a different story."

Her words, like sharp quills, invaded the king's heart. Angered, he said, "So be it."

The queen, too, could hardly restrain her anger. "Then say that with no ambiguity. Why be pretentious and hide behind false words? Being a king, are you afraid to voice the truth?"

The king answered, "Nobody ever wanted to know the truth from me. None can claim that I've been untruthful."

The queen replied, "Do you remember the day they were born?"

She paused, her words caught up in the web of time, as she travelled back almost twenty years, remembering that day.

The difference between the simple, trusting, young bride of yesteryears and today's middle-aged woman, neglected, exploited, devoid of husband's attention, was too great. The young Kamal Kumari of those days, who, after giving birth to her first born, had waited with love and patience for her husband to come, and to take her son in his arms, exulting in happiness. Expecting his arrival, she forgot the pains of childbirth and in her heart, there flowed a stream of bliss. But when the moments changed to minutes, and then to hours, and still the King did not come, she felt neglected and hurt. Dejected and sad, she heard the maidservant saying, "Queen Chanchal Kumari, too, has given birth to a prince around the same time. The king is with her and he has tied the amulet of immortality on the feet of her newborn. His Majesty will come here later."

It had been a tradition of the Royal house of Mewar that at the birth of the firstborn, the king tied the amulet of immortality on the tiny feet. It was a symbol, whereby the king declared his firstborn to be his successor. On hearing that the king had been unfair in putting the precious amulet on the feet of his younger prince, instead of his elder one, fierce fire swelled in Kamal Kumari's heart. The tears from a mother's eyes anointed the newborn on that day. The queen understood well that the seat of love in her husband's heart was no more reserved for her; her husband didn't love her anymore. In the past, too, such thoughts had assailed her, like frail doubts, but they never lasted long. She had reprimanded herself for doubting her husband. But, on that day, the temporary doubts took root as truth in her mind. Shell-shocked, the queen had felt like dying.

When her husband came to visit the newborn, she had not utterred a word. Within a few days, she had heard rumours within the palace walls, that claimed that because of the mistake made by the maidservants, who had miscalculated the birth time of Chanchal Kumari's firstborn, the king had tied the amulet on her boy, thinking him to be the eldest.

Kamal Kumari did not have the heart to judge the veracity of this rumour. She had no trust in the king's love for her, and his proximity became another cause of pain and agony for her. How on earth would one engage in such talks with him? Many a time, she'd attempted to broach this subject, to question him, and each time, her misery had been so immense that she came back, erasing the thoughts from her mind.

But after so many years, when she had almost no reason to disbelieve his very reason for tying the amulet on Jayasingha's feet, at his birth, her heart stomped out the wifely hurt from its crevices. It only reminded her she was Bhimsingha's mother and that he suffered only because he was born of her ill-fated womb. His luck forsook him, meting out grievous injustice to him, depriving him of his natural right. Deadly anger replaced hurt in her heart then.

She stood against the king, to fight for justice, to fight for her son's rights.

When the incidents around his birth flashed before her eyes, once again, it made her weaker; the fire of anger that lighted her eyes at once turned tearfully misty with the remembered hurt. But not for long. Soon enough, the queen, practicing complete self-restraint, spoke out angry words: "If you aren't afraid to speak the truth, then why could you not come up with the real reason of tying the amulet on the feet of your younger son, when all the while, it was your eldest son, who deserved it?"

Angered, the king replied, "It's not my duty to explain my decisions or the reasons behind them to the subjects. And if people misinterpret my actions, you can hardly blame me for that. Right? If I'd hidden the truth on that day, fearing the public backlash, then I'd have hesitated to give him the throne, even today. If people had any wrong assumptions, let this action of mine dismiss those forever. This is my kingdom, and I reserve the right of bestowing it to whomsoever I please; I'm neither afraid of the public and nor should they have any right to comment on this."

Unable to tolerate further, the queen stood up from her seat, and in an agitated voice, said, "No, don't you dare think like that, O King. It might be your kingdom, but you've no right to bestow it upon anyone you deem fit. You may be the judge, but that doesn't give you the right to be unjust. Your kingship doesn't give you the right to break laws. And if a King does that, then he's not a king–he is a despot, an unrighteous ruler. My son will not accept such a king's bounty. The day he claims this kingdom as his rightful domain, it'll be his. Even if you wish to give the kingdom to him now, he will not accept it from you. Remember this when your unfair decision results in bloodshed. It will take the lives of millions of innocent people, bringing huge destruction to this land. When bloodshed between brothers will bring the legacy of Mewar to ignominy, don't blame them or others. Do remember then, O king, that this is the consequence of your sin. You're the member of the lineage of the famous *Raghu clan* (One of the highest class of Kshatriya clan whose dynasty was named after the legendary king Raghu) , whose patriarch King Dashrath didn't hesitate to banish his favorite son Rama to forest, just to uphold justice. Despite being born into such an illustrious family, today, you defamed your family name. But, as long as this world exists, and the planets revolve, you cannot suppress justice with injustice; truth shall triumph, O king, you'd not be able to stop its march."

Deep hatred laced her words. Having spoken them out, the proud woman went out of the king's bedchamber, in slow, graceful steps. She didn't meet Bhimsingha that night and decided to have a talk with him the next morning.

2

The queen departed; she left behind a cacophony of censure and the words continued to target the Rana, like a thunderbolt. His mind echoed back the words of his queen: *"You are the member of the lineage of the famous Raghu clan, whose patriarch King Dashrath didn't hesitate to banish his favorite son Rama to forest..."* He felt dizzy from their onslaught; his majesty, the great Rana Raj Singha, became as restless as a small child. "Oh, what have I done? I've compromised truth at the feet of fraternal love, despite being born in a family that upheld truth at any cost. Oh God, was this the purpose of my unlucky birth, only to tarnish the unsullied name of my family?"

It was as if his closed eyes were suddenly open.

Never had he thought about the matter in this manner. In his mind, since Bhimsingha and Jayasingha, both were born on the same day, neither of them had precedence on the throne. It was his kingdom, and he thought to give it to whom he deemed fit. Blinded by one-sided love, he had, so far, failed to ponder upon the other aspect of the issue. But, today, he was cured of such illusion, such oversight, in a harsh way.

The night passed in a restless state. He could not sleep. At the crack of dawn, he said to the guard, "Ask Prince Bhimsingha to come here at once."

"Prince Bhimsingha?" The guard expressed surprise, for they all knew Jayasingha to be the crown prince. Suppressing his surprise, he went out to inform Bhimsingha.

That his father called to meet him surprised Bhimsingha no less. It was a novel occasion, for he could not remember ever to be called by the king, his father. He thought, *"Is this some new trick? Is he calling me to attend to Jayasingha, to be his servant? But does he not understand that, as long as Bhimsingha has faith in his own prowess and bravery, the throne would never be Jayasingha's."*

Remembering his father's partiality angered him afresh. He was in a dilemma. He pondered on how he could turn down the invitation to meet him. However, he decided not to disobey the royal command. *"Today, in his presence, I'm going to speak my heart out,"* he thought.

His heart seething with anger, Bhimsingha went to his father. But his anger melted as he glanced at the king who was looking for an escape route. Depression masked the king's face and his eyes, although troubled, were deep pools of love as he looked at Bhimsingha. Anger and revengeful feelings vanished in a moment; in its place, there was a strange emotion of unexpressed pain.

The king, too, was astonished to see Bhimsingha's calm, forbearing, respectful demeanor, just the very opposite of the image he'd conceived in his mind, in which Bhimsingha seethed with deep seated anger, frowning to demand fairness from him. Bhimsingha behaved like a loving son and to notice his respectful demeanour towards his father embarrassed the king. His son's respect, forbearance and calmness filled the king's heart with deep contrition, a feeling which no amount of anger on Bhimsingha's part would have aroused in the Rana's troubled heart. In deep shame and repentance, the king could not meet him in the eye.

Slowly, he said, "Son Bhimsingha!"

His affectionate tone surprised Bhimsingha. Never had the king expressed such tenderness for him. Slight and neglect had been his lot from his father. The memory of a day when both the brothers were playing in the garden invaded his consciousness; the king had caressed Jayasingha like a fond father, but for Bhimsingha he had spared not a word of endearment. Hurt with his behavior, the boy had left the place, found his mother's lap to shed his tears, without telling her the reason for his sorrow. Growing up, at every step, he'd observed the unfairness of his father. And by bestowing his throne to Jayasingha, he'd shown the height of unfairness. It had led him to believe, till now, that the king did not love him.

And so, after long years, when the king called him out, with such tenderness in his voice, it roused powerful emotions in his heart, overwhelming him. In a trembling voice, he replied, "Father."

All these years, Bhimsingha had addressed him as *Maharaja*, the king. Looking at him, the king confessed, "Son, I've wronged you in a deplorable way. Please forgive me."

Tears coursed down Bhimsingha's eyes, tears of hurt and pride. That his father realised and acknowledged his unfair behaviour towards him washed away his hurt. In his heart, he said, *"I've lost your affection, for I stayed away, aloof from you, doubting your affection for me. For this reason, I seek your forgiveness. Forgive me, father."*

He stood speechless in front of the king; the king, observing his silence, continued, "I know it is difficult for you to forgive me, but I'll atone for the crime I committed, and I ask forgiveness from my conscience, from my God. You're my firstborn; to you, shall I give my throne, on your head, the crown shall glitter. But even if I do so, on your path Jayasingha would always stand as a barrier, an impediment. It is because of my fault that he's dreaming of possessing that which is not his. The greed of the kingdom would turn him to cause anarchy in the land. And there is, but only one solution to this problem."

Saying so, he unsheathed the sword that glittered and shone bright against the rays of the sun. Holding it in front of Bhimsingha, he said, "Take this, and pierce this sword through his heart. Let one death ward-off thousands of deaths, let justice prevail at the downfall of injustice. Don't panic, on the face of cold responsibility. No relationship is important enough." His voice shook as he uttered the words, realising their onus within his heart.

Like a statue carved in stone, Bhimsingha stood. In a flash, he understood what the king was going through. To uphold his duty, he was sacrificing his most valuable loved treasure. Bhimsingha witnessed the intense loftiness of his father's ideals; his greatness impressed him to the core. His love for his father increased a thousand-fold. It was clear to Bhimsingh that by piercing the heart of his brother, he would, in fact, be stabbing his father. He could speak nothing; his mind only whispered, *"You're a god, a divine being."*

Watching him standing quietly, the king again reiterated, "Son, don't shiver at this thought. You'd be committing this act to uphold justice for the well-being of the land. There's no sin in this act of yours. And even if you commit a sin, it'd be not yours, it'd be mine. Follow my command and fulfil it."

Bhimsingha took the sword from his hand and kept it at the king's feet. He said, "Father, take back your sword. I've no need for it. You have indeed wronged me, but you've repented enough for it. You've fulfilled your duty to the letter. Now let me fulfil mine. I'll make sure that there will not be a drop of bloodshed because of me; that Jayasingha would commit nothing untoward because of me. The right that you've given me today, I grant that right to Jayasingha. From today onward, this kingdom shall rightfully be his. I'll leave Mewar to prevent myself from getting tempted, in the future, by the greed of attaining the throne. The affection and the lofty ideals that you imparted to me today, carrying those valuable treasures in my heart, I'll leave my motherland Mewar tonight. If I fail to do this, let me not be known as your son."

Not giving him a moment to respond or desist, Bhimsingha touched his father's feet and went away. Astounded, the king stood there.

That very day, Bhimsingha himself crowned Jayasingha. Then, along with his loved soldiers and nobles, he left Mewar. He never came back. Many years later, when his companions returned to Mewar, they carried with them the news of his death.*

*First published in the Borderless Journal

Swarnakumari Devi

Why?
Keno?

A woman devoid of her husband's love and attention, is such a woman known to be happy in this world? I'm indeed blessed. The Gods have adorned my motherly lap with a pretty, golden child and my mother-in-law is as affectionate as queen *Kaushalya* (Kaushalya was the eldest queen of King Dasaratha of Kosala. She was the mother of the Hindu god Rama) And yet, the fire rages in my bosom. My mother-in-law doesn't spare a moment advocating on my behalf whenever she meets her son. In so many ways, she tries to evoke the feelings of kindness in his heart for me. At times, she engages in admonishing him, too.

However, her efforts have yielded no results so far. My husband returns home at the end of the day. But my mother-in-law's admonition makes him go away; for a day or two he even disappears. That I'm not his object of love and attention is perhaps bearable; but those days when he stays away from our home, his absence becomes unbearably painful for me. His neglect and indifference appear to be much more acceptable to me than his empty absence. Yes, it is almost like I'm fed on addiction, very much like those compulsive users of alcohol or opium. And even though I have a full understanding of my situation, I'm unable to rid myself of this fixation. As a result, instead of appreciating my mother-in-law's sincere efforts in turning my husband's mind and heart towards me, I end up disapproving her lack of far-sightedness.

It is now almost a fortnight that he is absent from the home and the hearth. We have sent the messengers to his 'place' several times. His 'place' is locked, they tell us. 'The master has left for his *baganbari* (pleasure resort).' While the news worries my mother-in-law immensely, for me it brings along sleepless nights and an aversion for food. The day somehow passes, paying attention to my little boy, and praying nonstop to the Gods above.   Once, after I'd spent the entire night lamenting in tears, I fell into sleep towards the dawn. In my dream, the sky burst forth with golden hued light, and amidst the shimmering rays, I saw a woman with her visage like a goddess, seated on a throne of gold. Throwing a hibiscus flower at me, she said, "Take it and wear it on your crown. Your husband would love you dearly." As I held the flower, I woke up from my dream.

It was yet to be dawn. I rushed to my mother-in-law, and shared the dream with her. Hearing me out, she asked, "Dear, have you got that flower?"

"No," I told her.

"Dear one, go to the temple of Goddess Kali at *Kalighat* (The famous temple of the Hindu goddess Kali is situated in Kalighat, a locality in Kolkata) I believe it is Goddess Kali who came into your dream. Go to her temple and wear the flower offered to her."

2

Our home being in *Bhowanipore*, (A locality in the south of Kolkata) I've often visited the illustrious Kali temple, praying to the Goddess, sharing the pain in my heart. This morning, as I stood at her doorstep, my eyes resting on her fierce image, beside the river of blood trickling from the sacrifice of the animal, I felt dizzy. Tottering, I watched her protruding tongue, her sword yielding hands, her neck adorned with severed heads. It was impossible to find any resemblance to the kind, beatific, beautiful, vivacious Goddess of my dreams with this violent image of Kali. The vision in my dream had filled me up with optimism, tempering down my fears; but a glance at the image of Kali in front of me wove fear into my being, and I trembled as a feeling of hopelessness spread within me. I collapsed on her doorstep.

My lady servant, Umi Dasi, who had accompanied me to the temple, felt afraid, too. "Oh dear, what's wrong with our *mistress*!" she wailed.

A familiar priest, whom we knew well, poured some water on my head, with the ritualistic *Kosha-Kushi* (copper double spoon used to offer holy water to the Gods) and told Umi, "Take the lady and make her sit under that tree there. This place is too crowded with people coming and going."

Holding on to Umi, I walked out of the temple and sat under the shade of the solitary tree. Another lady was sitting there, too. Umi started chatting with her.

"I was so scared when my mistress fainted over there. So, where do you come from?"

The lady replied, "From faraway. You wouldn't know me. Where are you from?"

"We hail from Bhowanipore. You must have heard about Prannath babu. He used to be a man of goodness, but not anymore..." Umi answered.

"How is this lady related to him?"

"His wife, who else?" Umi answered back. "It's a

sad story. She's now the abandoned wife. He prefers the ugly one over her. He almost never pays a glance to her, and she, in utter sadness, is killing herself over that. If I ever get to see that wretched woman, I'd give her a piece of my mind. A witch, a heartless woman, she is! How she makes my good lady suffer! Anyway, gossip says that the other one once belonged to an honorable family... It's very unfortunate..."

Recovered by now, I said, "Why blame her, Umi? Destiny hadn't written happiness in my lot. Why blame her?"

Hearing me speak, the unfamiliar lady came closer. "You're as graceful as Goddess Lakshmi. Pity that your husband finds no value in you!"

Umi replied, "Not only that. He only comes to spend the night with her when he needs her ornaments. Look at my mistress! She wears not a string of gold on her body. So many times, we've cautioned her not to give away her ornaments. Let the man go. But each time he sweet talks to her, telling her about his troubles. She loses her mind listening to him and parts with her jewelries. The other day, her mother-in-law, warned him to bring back her daughter in-law's golden ornaments from the moneylender. He kept those as a pawn there. Ever since then, he is traceless. And my mistress is breaking her head and heart over him."

"Hush Umi! What're you blabbering?" I felt ashamed.

The lady said, "You're right, Umi. We would never have seen the face of such a husband. Good times must come into your life, dear one. A person as pure as you don't suffer forever."

The light of mercy kindled in her eyes. She took my hands in hers, coming closer to me. Her voice trembled as she said, "One who cannot value such a virtuous lady is an unfortunate soul. Dear one, give me all your sorrows, May the Goddess Kali shower happiness upon you."

Her visage glowed with a divine beauty. She almost resembled the Goddess of my dream.

That very afternoon, an unknown old woman came to our home. "Here you go mistress, take back your ornaments. Your husband had kept these with me when I loaned him some money. He has now paid me back and he asked me to give you back these ornaments."

In her happiness, my mother-in-law forgot to talk. Umi said, "Goddess Kali has transformed our babu's mind. Come mistress, come here..."

My mother-in-law supervised the ornaments. In a low voice, I asked the old woman, "When did he pay you?" I wished to know when she had met him. It brought peace, even if I knew that someone else had seen him.

The old woman replied, "Just today, I mean, just a few days back. But I couldn't come before."

My mother-in-law wanted to know when her son would return home.

The old woman became angry. "How do I know that? Now that you've got back your ornaments, I'll take my leave." I wished I could stop her for a while, and enquire a few more things. But she left in haste.

The members in our household rejoiced as my husband returned home that evening. My mother-in-law arranged for his meal, and as he took his seat to eat, she said, "Son, we got back all the ornaments, but we are all thrilled that God has blessed you with good sense."

Surprised, my husband stared at her. "Ornaments?"

"Why, the old woman to whom you had pawned your wife's ornaments today came to return those. She informed us you have repaid the money."

Taking a deep breath, he only said, "Oh!"

He finished his meal and came to my room. "You got back your ornaments? May I see them?" he asked.

I brought them to him. He rummaged through the pile. He appeared rather dull on that day; after combing through my ornaments, he seemed quite disconsolate.

His crestfallen face saddened me. I said, "Do you need these ornaments again? Please take them if you need them."

In a painful voice, he replied, "No."

Like other days, he left the room. I went to sleep, holding my child to my breast. My mind thought about my husband's woebegone face. I fell into a deep sleep, unlike other days. Early morning, my child's blabbering woke me up. But even after I woke up from the dream, I still felt being in that somnolent state. Rubbing my eyes, I wondered if what I saw was true. My husband stood nearby; his expression was quite somber. It was as if in his heart a great agitation was raging. Startled, I asked, "You! What is the matter?"

Without a word, he sat down on the bed and held our child close to his heart. Our son giggled, while tears coursed down the cheeks of my husband. Inconsolable, I cried out, "My lord, my husband, what is the matter? Tell me everything. I shall try to redeem your sorrow even if I have to pay it off with my life."

He put the baby on the bed and brought me closer to him. "Can you forgive me? I have nothing more to ask."

My eyes welled up with tears. I passed out in happiness. Such supreme bliss I had never experienced in my life. I learnt on that day that heaven existed on this earth, and the soul can experience the bliss of liberation, even being chained to this body.

From that very day, my husband transformed. He is now a householder, living with his wife and child.

But what is the reason behind this transformation? I am still very curious to know that.

He is unwilling to answer my question. Once, when I pressed hard, he said in a grievous voice, "Please do not ask me that, I beg of you." Ever since then, I've not raised that topic.

But in my mind, I always ask myself, "Why?"

To date, I have failed to come to a fixed conclusion. That is why, today, I am asking you all this question: Why? Why did it happen?

Bharati & Balak, Asadh, 1298

Rabindranath Tagore

Bolai
Bolai

It is often said that human life is a culmination of the various other life forms in this world. In our daily lives, most often, we come across diverse characteristics of other animals in a human being. Honestly said, in the life of a human, we see a blend of those characteristics prevalent in animals. The domesticity of a cow and the ferocity of a tiger reside in the same human; it is as if the snake and the mongoose are both put together. It is somewhat like the melody created when the entire range of notes come together. Only then, *'raga'*(A melodic framework and central feature of the classical Indian music tradition) is formed. However, within a 'raga', there can be the prominence of one note over the other.

In the character of my nephew Bolai, I believe the affinity for the flora and the fauna, perhaps, reigned supreme. He was an observant child rather than an active one. Even at an early age, he'd rather quietly observe Nature around him. The dark, billowing clouds in layers, on the eastern sky would collect and pour. It would moisten his heart and bring forth the untamed breeze of the forests. It was as if his entire being could hear the pitter-patter of the rains. In the departing light of the sun in the evening, he wanted to absorb it within, as if trying to accumulate something precious out of it. At the end of *Magh*, (the month of January) when the trees brimmed over with abundant tiny fruits, it awakened an intrinsic, deep happiness within him, a joy defying description. His inner nature would blossom forth, expand and take on a deeper shade of color, much like those flowering Sal trees, with the arrival of *Falgun (the month of February)*. In those moments, he had a deep urge to sit in solitude, engaged in a conversation with himself, piecing together the various tales he'd heard. Like the story of that ancient pair of birds who had made their nest in the deep crevice of the ancient banyan tree. He never talked much, this wide-eyed, staring boy. In the silence of his being, his thoughts ran deep.

Once, I took him along on a trip to the mountains. His joy was immense when he saw the lush carpet of the green grass sprawling down to the valley from our house at the top. In his mind, the grass carpet on the slope was not an inanimate, lifeless thing; he felt it to be a living one that rolled down in a playful manner. Often, he would roll down the slope, becoming a part of the grass, enjoying it tickling his back, and giggled out aloud.

After a rain-washed night, when the first gentle rays of sun broke free, and its golden light kissed the tops of the clustering *deodar* trees, he would tip-toe out of home, alone, walk to those tall trees, and stand in awe, watching the motionless mighty trunks. In them, he'd envision a living spirit, a human presence. The spirits who wouldn't talk but would know all our secrets. Like our ancestral grandfathers, from the time immemorial.

His deep-thinking eyes weren't always heavenwards; many a time, I'd seen him roaming in my garden, his eyes down on the soil, as if searching for something there. His curiosity knew no bounds when he discovered those new seedlings growing up through the soil. Each day, bending down, he would talk to them, as if asking, "What's next? Now what?" Those were like his incomplete stories. Like those new, tender leaves, with whom he shared a strange affinity, verging on companionship.

And they, too, would be eager to ask him questions. Perhaps they ask him his name. Or, about his mother, where was she? In his mind, Bolai would reply, "But I don't have a mother."

When someone plucked a flower from the tree, it hurt him. He realized soon enough that his concern or hurt is not at all important to others. He tried to hide his pain. When the young boys of his age threw stones at the trees, trying to bring down the *amlokis* (gooseberries) from the tree top, he escaped from that scene. To tease him further, his companions would walk through the garden, thrashing the row of shrubs on both sides with their sticks; they would tear the branch of the *bakul* (Minnesap species) tree. He felt like crying, but couldn't, only because others might think him to be mad. The worst day in his life came when the grasscutter came to mow the grass in the garden.

For he'd seen the small tendrils of creepers rousing their heads within the patch of grass, and those purple-yellow tiny nameless flowers embedded with them. Here and there, the 'kantakari' (wild eggplant) shrubs, with small bluish flowers sported a speck of gold in their hearts. Those creepers of 'kalmegh' (bitter medicinal plant) near the fence borders, and the 'anantamul' (a medicinal plant) displayed their leaves. The sprouting *neem* that blossomed forth out of the seeds dropped by the birds. How beautiful they looked! And the cruel grasscutter machine brutally mowed all these over. There's nobody to listen to their plea or protest, for these are not the most sought-after plants in the garden.

Some days, Bolai would come to his aunt, sit on her lap and wrapping his small arms around her neck, would only say, "Why don't you ask those grass-cutters not to kill my plants?"

Aunt replied, "Bolai, don't be a fool. These overgrown plants are weeds, almost like a jungle. We must clean these."

Bolai had by then understood that there were some pains, some sorrows, that were only his own; those never moved others.

Bolai probably was born in that age and time, when the universe first swam out of the womb of the ocean, taking its first breath, eons of years ago. At a time, when on the newly formed layers of mud, the nascent forests rose and gave out their first cry. Then, there were no birds, no sound, no life, only layers of rocks, slime and water. Those tall trees, heralding other life forms on the path of Time, called out to the glowing sun, with their raised hands, saying, *"I'll live, I'll exist, I'll survive, like the eternal traveler, through the cycles of death, through days and nights, rain and shine, I'll progress on the path of my growth, my evolution."* Those murmurings of the trees still reverberate, through the forests and the hills; on the tendrils of their leaves the life force of earth murmurs, *"I'll live, I'll exist."* These mute trees, like foster mothers of the earth, have milked the heavens for endless time, to gather life nectar, its radiance, for this earth. And, they raise their endless eager heads to the air, expressing their soul's call, saying, *"I'll live."* In some strange, miraculous way, Bolai could hear that calling in the blood that coursed through him. The very thought had made us laugh.

One fine morning, as I was reading the newspaper, Bolai came up and took me to the garden. Pointing out to a small shrub, he asked me, "Uncle, what's that plant?"

It was a small shoot of a *simul* (silk cotton) tree, arising through the crack of our gravel road.

Bolai had made a mistake by bringing me there. The sapling was a tiny one, just like the first babbling of a child; it was then that Bolai had noticed it. Thereafter, Bolai had himself tended to the plant, watering it, checking it up to see its growth each morning and evening.

Silk cotton plant, although grew fast, yet it seemed not to keep pace with Bolai's eager wait. When it grew to a certain height, by observing the beauty of its rich leaves, Bolai was certain it was a tree of a special kind. His observation was quite similar to that of a mother who, after observing the first hint of intellect in a child, marks it to be a child of wonder. Bolai, too, had thought that he'd astonish me with his tree.

I said, "I've to tell the gardener to uproot the tree."

Bolai was aghast. Those were quite terrible thoughts for him. He said, "No Uncle, I beg of you, please don't get it uprooted."

"I truly don't understand you," I told him. "That tree stands right in the middle of the path. Once it grows, it'll spread cotton all over. It'll be a nuisance."

Bolai realized it was no use arguing with me. The motherless boy then went to his aunt. Sitting on her lap, with his arms around her neck, he sobbed. "Aunt, please tell uncle, so that he may not uproot the tree."

His plan worked. His aunt called me and said, "Oh listen, please let his plant be."

I let it be. Had he not shown the sapling to me, I would have not have noticed it. But now, I noticed it every day. Within a year, the tree grew taller shamelessly. As for Bolai, he reserved his best adoration for this tree.

The tree continued to grow in a ridiculous manner, paying no respect at all to anyone around. It grew to its full height, standing on that inappropriate spot. Whoever saw it wondered at its being there. Twice more I proposed for uprooting it. I tempted Bolai with my offer of nice, high quality rose saplings. I also proposed, "If you still opt for the silk-cotton tree, then let me get you a fresh sapling. We can plant it next to the fence. It'll look pretty there."

But any talk of uprooting it alarmed Bolai. And his aunt said, "Oh, it doesn't look that bad there."

When Bolai was an infant, my sister-in-law had passed away. The grief, perhaps, made my elder brother careless; he went abroad to study engineering. Motherless, this child grew up in my childless home, in the lap of his aunt, my wife. Ten years later, my brother returned from abroad and took Bolai to Shimla to impart western education to him. Later, he planned to take Bolai abroad.

Bolai was inconsolable as he left our home, turning it into an empty house.

Two years passed. During this time, Bolai's aunt, saddened by his absence, dried her tears in solitude, and spent her time in Bolai's room, arranging and rearranging a single torn shoe he wore, a damaged rubber ball he played with and that picture book of animals. She wondered if Bolai must have outgrown all these by now.

In between, the wretched silk cotton tree continued to grow; so tall it had grown that it was now mandatory to cut it down. I chopped it down one day.

Soon after this, Bolai's letter reached us from Shimla. "Aunt, send me a photograph of my silk-cotton tree."

Before leaving for abroad, Bolai was supposed to

come and meet us once. But that now cancelled, Bolai wished to take his friend's photograph along.

His aunt called me, saying, "Listen, please bring a photographer."

I asked, "Why?"

She showed me the letter in Bolai's childish handwriting.

I said, "That tree has already been chopped off."

Bolai's aunt didn't touch food for the next couple of days and stopped communicating with me for even longer. When Bolai's father had taken him away from her, it was the severing of her umbilical cord; but when Bolai's uncle uprooted Bolai's favorite tree forever, it shattered her world and deeply wounded her heart.

For that tree was, to her, a reflection of Bolai, his substitute image.*

*First published in Borderless Journal

Rabindranath Tagore

Subha

Subha

When the girl was christened as Subhashini, who knew that she would be dumb? Her parents named the two elder sisters as Sukeshini and Suhashini. The father honored the request to rhyme the name of his youngest daughter to his elder ones. He named her as Subhashini. Thereafter, in was shortened into Subha.

After a lot of research and spending quite a lot of money, her parents married off their two elder daughters; the youngest one, now, was like a burden, filling the hearts of her parents.

Few realized the fact that, although she could hardly communicate, she had deep feelings. Not understanding this, people spoke about her misfortune, in her presence, worrying about her future. At a very tender age, it dawned upon her that her birth in her father's house was nothing but a curse. Therefore, she always hid herself away from the sight of the commoners, staying on the sidelines. In her mind, the words reverberated, *I wish they forgot me!* But alas! Like a persistent pain in their heart, her parents did not forget her presence.

It was her mother, who especially looked upon her as an aberration of herself: a mother always viewed her daughter as an extension of her own self. If the daughter lacked in any area, it became a cause of shame for her. Subha's father, Banikantha, however, loved Subha a bit more than his other daughters; but in her mother's eyes, she was a shameful reminder of her womb. As such, she had little love lost for Subha.

Subha lacked words. She could not talk, but she had a pair of dark, large, deep-pooled eyes and her lips trembled like fragile leaves whenever a thought arose in her mind.

When we express ourselves with words, the expressions bear our own stamp; it is quite similar to translation, in a way. It is not always accurate and with our inability to express, at times, we err. But no words are needed to translate a pair of dark eyes-mind itself lends them a meaning of its own. In their depths, thoughts rise and fall, shining brightly or shrinking in light, holding a steadfast gaze, like the setting moon or like the restless scattering away of the strains of lightning. The one for whom there existed no other expression, other than the ones that flitted across her face. It was a wonder to know that the language of her eyes was abysmally deep. Much like the clear sky, where light and shadow played eternally. There existed a grandeur, as deep as Nature, in these silent, mute personas. Afraid of her silence, normal children refused to play with her. Subha was alone and speechless, very much like the lonely afternoons.

2

Chandipur-that was the name of the village, where Subha lived. A river flew by the village, a small river of Bengal, respecting its boundary, much like the daughters of the middle-class families. The not so broad, svelte river flew industriously, protecting its banks; it was as if she shared a relation with the villagers living on both sides of her shaded shores. A little below the village, the river trotted in happiness, like a village goddess, and carried forth her numerous works of goodwill with grace.

Right there, looking out at the river, was Banikantha's home. No boatmen, passing that way, could miss his small hut, stacked with hay, encircled by the tamarind grove, and the orchard of mango, jackfruit, and banana. I don't know if, amidst this material richness, anyone had any eye for the dumb girl, but in her free time, having finished her chores, she often would come and sit by the river bank.

It was as if the loving Nature spoke on behalf of her, compensating her lack of speech. The babbling of the brook, the noise of the people, the song of the boatmen, the rustling of leaves all came together, mingling with the back and forth of our entire existence. Like a wave, it splashed across the shore of her heart. Like the various sounds and movement in Nature, this too, was the language of silence. And it was also the language of Subha, Subha with her deep-pooled, dark eyes, shaded by long lashes. From the chirping crickets in the grassland to the silent, sprawling space between the constellations, there were only allusions, signs, music, moans and whispers, for her.

And in the midday, when the boatmen and the fishermen, went away for their meal, the householders enjoyed their siesta, when the birds fell silent for a while and the ferry boats stopped their service, when the entire world seemed to pause amid all works, and fell quiet, like a lonesome giant, then under that vast heavenly sky, there sat in silence a mute girl facing a dumb Nature- one resting under the boundless sunlight and the other, under the shade of a small tree.

Subha had a handful of intimate friends. Sorboshi and Panguli, the two cows at the stable, recognized her by her footsteps, even though they never heard her call out their name. In her murmurings, there was a gentleness, which they felt and understood much better than any language. When she petted them, or scolded them, or even pleaded with them, those cows understood her feelings better than the humans.

Inside the stable, Subha would put her arms around Sorboshi's neck, rub her cheek against the cow's ears and Panguli would look at them, with her kind eyes, and licked her with love. Thrice a day, Subha would visit the stable; and then there were those irregular visits. She would most surely come visiting these two mute friends whenever they rebuked her harshly at home. By some unusual sense of inference, they could fathom the pain in the girl's heart from the look of anguish on her face. Coming closer to Subha, they'd rub their horns against her arms, trying to bring comfort to her silent distress.

Other than the two cows, there was also a goat and a kitten, but with them, Subha did not share the same level of friendship, although that did not stop them from showing their allegiance to her. The kitten occupied her warm lap, irrespective of day or night, and there it slept; and, when Subha ran her soft fingers over its neck and back, it did not forget to show that her soothing massage, especially helped him in courting sleep.

3

Among the higher species, Subha also gained another mate, but the nature of the relation that she shared with him was difficult to surmise. The reason was because he could speak. As a result, there was no common language among them.

His name was Pratap. He was the youngest son of the Gosain family. Lazy that he was, his parents had given up all hopes that anyone would ever employ him for any work. Such idle people had an enormous advantage. Although they would earn the irk of their relatives, others would often love them. They became almost like public property, as no work bound them strictly. Just as a city must have a few public gardens, where people would come together, for a breathing space, in the same way, every village must also have a few people of leisure. In times of need, be it for work or for entertainment, they always came in handy.

Pratap loved fishing, as it helped him idle away a lot of his time. Most of the afternoons, he'd be seen engaged in this activity. Because of this, his meetings with Subha were most frequent. Pratap always felt good when he had her company, no matter which task he'd be engaged with. A silent, mute companion was indeed the best one to have while fishing. Pratap understood that and hence he respected Subha for that. And so, while everyone called her Subha, Pratap showered more affection on her by calling her as "Su".

While Subha would sit under the tamarind tree further away, Pratap would sit on the ground and stare at the water, angling for the fish with his fishing line. While fishing, Pratap chewed *paan (betel leaf)*, which Subha prepared for him. And, by doing so, perhaps she wished to make it clear to him, by her long gaze, that she, too, was a useful person in this world, who might be of some help to him. But she could not do anything else. Then, in her mind, she turned to the divine, chanting silently for a miraculous power that would enable her to perform something so extraordinary that might surprise Pratap. And, he would say, "Goodness! I'd no inkling that our Şuvi possessed such abilities!"

Imagine, if Subha was a mermaid; slowly, rising out of the water, she would place the jewel of the snake's crown beside the bank and Pratap, dismissing away his miserable fishing, would dive into the river, along with the jewel. Reaching the netherworld, he would discover the princess sitting on the golden throne in the silvery palace. Who else could it be, but the mute daughter of Banikantha-our Subha? Could our "Su" not be the sole princess of that deep, quiet, brightly jeweled city? Was it so impossible to be true? Nothing is, in fact, impossible, and yet instead of being born in the royal family of the netherworld, Su was born in Banikantha's family, having no means to amaze Pratap, the son of the Gosain's.

4

Subha grew up as time passed. Slowly, she discovered her own self. It was as if that a wave of tide from the depth of some unknown sea, on a full-moon night, splashed her inner being. Her soul brimmed over with a nameless consciousness. It was time to think and discover herself, question herself; but she found no answers.

On a deep full-moon night, she would open the doors of her bedroom, looking out, with fearful eyes. Nature, bathed in full moon light, as lonely as Subha, sat awake, looking down at the sleepy earth below. Ecstasy and misery ran through Subha, saturating her, in her loneliness, and coursed even beyond, unspoken, unspeakable. The mute girl stood in silence at the fringes of Nature's world and she felt troubled.

As she grew up, the thoughts of her marriage started

preying hard on the minds of her parents. People around criticized her parents, threatening them to make them an outcast in the village, if they didn't get their daughter married soon. Banikantha was an affluent man, he could afford to have a meal of rice and fish every day, and hence he also had enemies.

After a prolonged discussion with his wife, Bani left the village for a while. While returning, he said, "Let's go to Calcutta."

As the preparation began for their departure, Subha's heart filled with wisps of tears, like a morning breathing in fog. An unknown fear made itself known in her bosom and, like a dumb animal, she skirted around her parents; her large eyes scanned their faces, trying hard to comprehend something, but they'd not be forthcoming.

One afternoon, while casting the fishing line in water, Pratap said with a laugh, "Why, Su, they've found a bridegroom for you, you're going to get married. Don't forget us, mind you!" And saying that, he concentrated on fishing.

Just as a heart-struck doe stares at the hunter and, in silence implores the hunter, 'How did I wrong you,', with such an expression in her eyes, Subha stared at Pratap. That day, she didn't sit under the tree. His afternoon siesta over, Banikantha was enjoying a drag of tobacco in his bedroom. Sitting next to his feet, Subha broke down into tears, her eyes fixed upon his face. And, trying to console her, Banikantha's eyes too teared up, wetting his cheeks.

On the morrow, they left for Calcutta. Subha visited the stable to bid adieu to her childhood friends. Feeding them with her own hands, she put her hands around their neck, gazing at them and, with her eyes brimming with tears, spoke to them. Tears coursed down her two eyes.

That night, when the moon was on its twelfth day of the fortnight, walking out of her room, Subha reached the riverside, her favorite place. There, under the glorious moon, she threw herself on the soft grassy bed. It was as if, with her two arms, she wished to hold her mute, Mother Earth, imploring to her, *"Oh, don't let me leave, Mother. Hold me tight, Ma, as I'm trying to hold you, and keep me here."*

One fine day, Subha's mother dressed her up in their Calcutta home. Her hair was tightly pulled back, tied with ribbons, and she was decked up with heavy ornaments. With this, her mother managed to kill her natural loveliness. As tears ran down Subha's eyes, her mother, afraid that it might give her eyes a swollen look, scolded her. But alas! the tears had no ears for her rebuke.

With a friend in tow, the bridegroom himself came for bride-viewing. Subha's parents, worried and alarmed, they fussed and bustled, as if God himself had arrived to select the beast of sacrifice. From the backstage, her mother volleyed out many instructions, which only increased the flow of Subha's tears, as she came and stood before the prober.

After examining her for long, the bridegroom declared, " Well, not so bad."

Observing the girl's tears, he deduced she was of a tender heart and concluded that if she felt sad, at the thought of bidding farewell to her parents, why, such a sensitive heart must surely be a possession worthy for him in the future. Like the pearl in the oyster, her teardrops increased her worth, but further argued nothing more on her behalf.

The marriage took place in an auspicious moment as decreed by the almanac.

Having delivered the dumb girl into someone else's

hands, her parents left for their village. And thanks to the Lord, it saved them from being an outcast in their village community.

The groom took Subha to the place where he worked, in the west part of the country.

Within a week, everyone understood that the new bride could not speak, that she was dumb. But if anyone had trouble understanding the obvious, could we blame Subha for that? For she had deceived no one, her eyes had spoken about everything; but none had comprehended her truth. Around herself, she found no words. Her eyes searched for the familiar faces, those who understood her mute language, ever since her birth and breath. In her silent heart, there arose an inexpressible, unending wail. Nobody heard it but her God.

Later, her husband, after duly inspecting with his eyes and ears, brought a new bride home- one who had the gift of the language and could talk.

MAGH, 1299

Sarat Chandra Chatterjee

Ramlal's Transformation
Ramer Sumoti

Ramlal was quite young, but his young mind was rather mischievous. Everyone in the village feared him. No one knew from where, when, and how his next move would come. His elder brother Shyamlal, who was his stepbrother, could also not be termed as a gentle person, but he did not believe in extreme punishment for minor errors. He worked at the landlord's estate office in the village and looked after his agricultural lands as well. They were rather affluent. He had some savings as cash, other than his possessions of ponds, gardens, rice fields, and a few houses of tenants, belonging to the *bagdi* caste (member belonging to the caste of field laborers). When Shyamlal's wife, Narayani, for the first time arrived at her husband's home, as the lady of the house, some thirteen years ago, Ram's widowed mother passed away. On her deathbed, she had entrusted her two-and-a-half-year-old son Ramlal, and her household, to the care of her new daughter-in-law Narayani. Narayani was only thirteen years old.

That year a strange fever raged throughout the village. Narayani, too, fell ill. Partially qualified Doctor

Nilmoni Sarkar was the only doctor for the three or four villages around. His fee now leaped up from one to two rupees, and his packets of quinine, added with arrowroot powder and flour, became delicious products! Seven days passed, but Narayani's fever did not subside. Shyamlal grew concerned.

The maid servant of the house, Nrityakali, went out to summon the doctor. Coming back, she declared, "The doctor must go to some other village today. There they would pay him four rupees. He can't come here."

Shyamlal felt angry. He said, "I shall also pay him four rupees. What comes first- money or life? Bring that rogue of a doctor!"

Narayani had overheard this conversation from inside her room. In a weak voice, she said, "Why are you getting so worked up, dear? Let the doctor come tomorrow. A day's delay wouldn't make much difference."

Ramlal was sitting under a guava tree, under their courtyard, and was busy making a cage for the birds. Getting up from there, he said, "You wait Netya, I'll go to the doctor."

Worried to hear her yong brother-in-law's voice, Narayani sat up on her bed. "Please stop him from going there," she called out to her husband. "Ram, dear one, my brother, don't go for heaven's sake, don't start a fight again, please."

Ram had no ears for her pleadings, and he went out. His five-year-old nephew Gobind had been holding the sticks for him. "Aren't you going to make the cage, uncle?" he asked.

"Will do it later." Saying so, Ram walked out.

Beating her forehead, Narayani addressed her husband, her voice almost broken with tears, "Why did you allow him to go? I fear what mischief he is going to commit now."

As it is, Shyamlal was already angry and peeved. Irked, he replied, "What can I do? He didn't listen to you. Why would he listen to me?"

"Why didn't you hold him back?" Narayani insisted. "Oh, he'd one day be the reason for my death, the wretched creature! Netya, don't stand there like that, dear! Get Bhola, and send him to placate Ram, and bring him back. Bhola perhaps hasn't yet taken the cows to the fields."

Nrityakali left in search of Bhola.

Ramlal reached the house of Doctor Nilmoni. He was in his dispensary, sitting at a decrepit table, facing a broken almirah, and he was busy weighing the medicine. Three or four patients were watching him, open-mouthed. Glancing at Ram from the side of his eyes, the doctor paid attention to his own work.

After a moment's silence, Ram asked, "Why isn't my sister-in-law getting better?"

The doctor kept his eyes fixed on the weighing scale. He said, "What can I do? I'm giving her medicines."

"What rubbish you're giving. How do you think rotten flour would cure her fever?"

Hearing this, Nilmoni glared at Ram, forgetting everything about the weighing and the scales. He was speechless with anger. That anybody in this world would be so audacious to utter such harsh words was beyond his belief.

A little later, he thundered back. "Oh really, rotten flour, is it? Why do you come to take the rotten flour, pray? Why does your brother request me to come and visit, then?"

"There are no doctors in this area, that is why," replied Ram. "Otherwise, he wouldn't have requested you."

People sitting there listened in stupefied silence. Glancing at them once, Ram continued, "You're a rather lowly person. You don't know how to show respect to the Brahmin. That is why you said that my brother fell at your feet and implored you to come. My brother doesn't crawl before anyone. When I was coming here, my sister-in-law made me promise, otherwise, I would have punched out your teeth before going back home. Now, listen carefully, take the best medicine, and come at once. If the fever doesn't go down, I shall chop away those mango saplings you've planted out there in your garden- they are quite young, still- not one of those will be there tomorrow, I'll hack them away with one strike of my axe. And tomorrow I shall come again and smash down all your bottles."

Warning in this manner, he went out.

The doctor remained stiffly seated in his seat.

"Don't delay, doctor," said an elderly patient, with some courage. "Carry the best medicines with you. He is Ram-Thakur. He won't rest until he carries out his threat."

Putting down the scales, the doctor said, "I am going to report this to the police inspector at the police station. You all are my witnesses."

The old man who had been advising so far, replied, "Witness? Who is going to come up with proof, doctor? My ears are buzzing after taking that dose of quinine. I could not even understand what Ram was saying. And what will the inspector do, sir? That boy Ram might be small, but his group of boys is not small at all. If they put fire to our homes, the inspector will not come to help, nor will he oblige us by bringing a bale of hay. We can't do anything. Everybody is afraid of him. It is better that you do what he has said. Please check my pulse now, doctor- tell me what I am supposed to eat today- flat bread or something?"

The doctor was fuming from inside; now, at the prospect of checking the pulse, he burst forth in anger. "If you all refuse to be my witness, why, then get lost from here, all of you. I will check no one's pulse, nor will I give medicines anymore, even if you all die. Let me see how you all fare!"

Holding the stick in hand, the old man got up to leave. "It is not your fault, doctor. He is a devil. But we must, at least, inform him, otherwise he might think that we've advised you to go to the police station. I've planted a few brinjals in my field and they are growing well. Who knows, he might pull them all out by tonight! His group of *bagdi* boys does not seem to sleep at night! Sir, you may go to the police station some other day; first take a bottle of medicine and pacify him."

The old man went away, and others too left. Nilmoni heaved a deep sigh, and reminded himself of the ultimate words of wisdom as learnt from the human experiences, before he got up, and went inside. 'One must not do any good for others,' he uttered.

Narayani's anxious eyes looked outside as she waited. Returning home, Ram called out for his nephew. "Gobind, come, and hold up the cage."

"Ram, come here," called Narayani.

With utmost care, Ram was putting the sticks in the bamboo frame. He replied, "Not now. I'm doing some work."

"Come right now, I say," scolded Narayani.

Keeping the sticks down, Ram went inside Narayani's room, and sat near the foot of her bed. Narayani asked, "Did you meet the doctor?"

"Yes."

"What did you tell him?"

"Asked him to come."

Narayani wanted to know the truth. "Tell me, what did you tell him?"

"No, I won't."

Nrityakali came inside the room and informed that the doctor was coming.

Pulling the thick blanket over herself, Narayani changed her side on the bed. Ram ran out of the room. A little later, the doctor came in, accompanied by Shyamlal. After finishing his examination of the patient, the doctor addressed to Narayani. "Curing the fever is not in the hands of the physician, dear. Your brother-in-law has given me only two days to cure you. If I do not cure you within these two days, he shall put my home on fire."

Ashamed to hear his words, Narayani replied, "That is how he is, doctor. Don't be afraid."

The doctor went on. "People say that he has a group. And they do what they say. That makes me scared, dear. We can give medicines, but we can't give life."

Keeping quiet, Narayani said, "That lad will land up in prison one day. I am afraid I too may have to follow him there."

Nilmoni had brought fresh quinine and authentic medicines from his medicine box. After giving them, as he was about to leave, Shyamlal offered him four rupees as his fee. Biting his tongue, the doctor exclaimed, "No, no, my fee is only one rupee. I can't accept more- I never do that, that's not me. Shyam babu, money is temporary, but one's *dharma (The Hindu concept of righteousness)* is perennial."

The doctor forgot conveniently that in that very house, just a couple of days back, he had accepted more than a rupee, as his fee. But Shyamlal understood everything.

In the meantime, Narayani recovered from fever. And life continued as before.

2.

A couple of months later, one day Narayani returned home, after having her bath in the river. Keeping down the pitcher filled with water, she asked Netya, "Netya, where is that monkey gone?"

Everyone in the house knew who the monkey was!

Netya replied, "The young master was here a while ago- there he is, making a kite."

Seeing him there, Narayani beckoned him. "Come here, you wretch, come soon," she called out. "Do you think I should hang myself, worrying about you?"

Ram was busy extracting the sticky glue from the half-broken wood apple by poking at it with a bamboo stick. Hearing her call, he came and stood near her.

Narayani asked, "Why did you chop down the entire rack of cucumber plants of the Santras, tell me?"

"Have they seen me doing that?"

"No, they haven't. But I have seen you. Why did you do that?"

"Why did they insult me?"

Angered, Narayani asked, "We will talk about the insult part later- you tell me, why were you stealing the cucumbers?"

It surprised Ramlal to hear that and he became annoyed. "Stealing? Absolutely not! I was only taking a small bit of cucumber; can you call that stealing?"

Enraged, Narayani replied, "Yes, of course, that is stealing! A hundred times stealing! Even that small baby there knows what stealing is! Go, and stand there on one leg, you rascal!"

In that house, Ram's nephew Gobind was the 'small baby' and he was Ram's pet. Gobind was always with him, and he helped Ram in all his works. Following Ram's orders, he had been, so far, holding the kite for him. Hearing the commotion, he left the kite and came and stood near his mother.

Observing Ram's hesitation, he quickly said, "Uncle, stand on one leg- like this." Saying so, he lifted his one leg, and showed him the technique of doing the job.

Ram gave a tight, resounding slap on his cheek, and turning his back, stood on his one leg.

Narayani stifled her laughter, and picking up her son, entered the kitchen. After a couple of minutes, when she returned, she saw Ram was still standing on his one leg, and was drying his tears with the end of his *dhoti* (A type of loose sarong, a lower garment worn by men in the Indian subcontinent.)

She walked closer to him, and pulled his arm, but he strutted, and with greater force, pushed her arm away. Smiling, she tried to pull his arm once again, but he wrenched himself free of her grip, and dashed away from there.

An hour later, Nrityakali came to call him. She saw Ramlal sitting in the temple courtyard against a pillar.

Nrityakali asked, "Is it not time for your school, young master?"

Ram did not answer him, and pretended not to hear her at all.

Coming in front, Netya said, "The mistress has asked you to take a bath and finish eating."

"Get lost," said Ram, seething with anger.

"But have you heard what the mistress has said?"

"No, I haven't. I won't take a bath, I won't have food, I won't do anything. You go away."

"I'll surely tell her that", said Nrityakali, and proceeded to leave.

Hearing it, Ram at once jumped up, and dashed towards the dirty pond in the back yard. He took a dip in it, and then sat down with his wet hair and wet clothes. When Narayani heard this, worried, she came rushing. "What a terrible boy you are! Look what you have done! Nobody dares to put even a foot in that dirty pond. And you took a dip in it!"

She dried his hair with her *aanchal*, changed his wet clothes, and served him meal. Ram sat there, his face crestfallen, and refused to touch his food.

Narayani very well understood his wish. Coming closer to him, she put her hand on his head, and said, "Dear brother, please eat yourself now. In the evening, I shall feed you with my own hands. See, I have not yet finished my cooking. Eat up now, dear boy."

Ram finished his meal, and putting on his shirt, he left for school.

"It is because of you he's getting spoiled, mistress," Nrityakali blamed Narayani. "Why must you feed such a big boy with your own hands? Why must you feed him always just because he is upset? Utter nonsense!"

Smiling slowly, Narayani replied, "Otherwise he won't eat. If I had not coaxed him saying I shall feed him the evening meal, he would have continued to sit here in a dejected manner, without eating."

Nrityakali replied, "Without eating.... oh, he would have eaten when hungry. He's a big boy..."

Dissatisfied to hear this, Narayani countered, "You all only see his age. When he grows up, and is wiser, do you think he would want to sit on my lap and like to be fed? He would feel ashamed then."

Peeved, Nrityakali said, "I say this for his own good, mistress. Why else should I mind? If he is no wiser at the age of twelve-thirteen, pray, when will he be wiser?"

Now Narayani got angry. "Netya, everybody doesn't mature with wisdom at the same time. Some have it two years earlier, some two years later," she retorted. "And whether or not he gets wiser- why are you all so bothered?"

Netya answered back. "That is the trouble with you, mistress. You can very well see it for yourself how unruly he has become. Neighbors says it is because of your pampering---"

"Neighbors can only see that I pamper him, but they have no eyes for the harsh punishment I give him," said Narayani in a rough voice. "But you are not one of those neighbors. He stood for the entire morning on one leg, took a dip in that dirty pond. God forbid, suppose he gets a fever! And then, you people wish I send him without food to school, is that it? I'm sick and tired of hearing such aspersions at home and outside, Netya." Words got choked in her throat as she spoke. Tears welled up in her eyes, and she wiped them away with her *aanchal*.

Netya, of course, was unaware of the fact that Narayani had had a quarrel with her husband the previous night on this very issue. Feeling ashamed and sad, she said, "Why are you crying, mistress? I'm not saying anything bad. People talk, I wanted to caution you a bit."

Wiping her tears, Narayani said, "God has not made everyone in the same way. I tolerate everything that people say, just because he is mischievous. But why must they accuse me of pampering him? What do they want? That I cut him into pieces and let him float away in the river? Perhaps then they'd feel happy." Not waiting for a response, she walked away.

Belittled, Nrityakali grumbled to herself. "I cannot understand, someone as intelligent and as patient as her, why cannot she understand this small fact? And what a punishment! For just a minute he stood on one leg and cried, and the mistress behaves as if it is the end of the world."

Ram disliked having meal with his brother. That evening, Narayani served the meals of the two brothers side by side deliberately and sat a bit further away from them. The moment Ram saw the arrangement entering the room, he jumped up. "I will not eat, no way I'm going to eat."

In a somber voice, Narayani said, "Then go to bed."

Ram stopped his agitation at hearing her serious voice, but he did not sit down to eat; in silence, he waited there.

The moment Shyamlal entered the kitchen through the other door, Ram dashed out of the room. Shyamlal sat down to eat. "Isn't Remo going to eat?" he asked.

"He'll have his dinner with me," replied Narayani, keeping it short.

Shyamlal finished his meal and left the room. At once, Ram entered the room, his fist full of ash. "I shall let no one eat today. I shall sprinkle ash over everyone's food, shall I do that?"

Looking up, Narayani said, "Just try that once, you'll then see the fun."

Ram changed his tone, hearing her warning. Holding the ash still in his fist, he said, "Very funny, in the morning you just tricked me into eating rice by myself. And now you must watch the fun."

"Why did you eat in the morning then?"

"You said in the evening you would..."

"Aren't you ashamed of being fed by someone else? You're a big boy, aren't you?"

Surprised, Ram said, "What do you mean by someone else? You yourself said you'd feed me."

Not willing to argue anymore, Narayani said, "Very well, now go, throw the ash, and wash your hands. But don't ask for this again."

Narayani was still feeding Ram, when Nrityakali glanced inside the room from the doorstep, for no reason at all, and then walked away to the other side of the verandah.

Observing that, Narayani said, "Ram, are you never going to calm down, brother? Will God never give you some wisdom? I'm tired of listening to the remarks of the people."

Gulping down the rice in his mouth, Ram said, "Who is the person? Give me his name."

"Yes, as if that solves everything," she said with a deep sigh.

However, after a few months, the situation became truly unbearable for Narayani.

Her widowed mother, Digambari, and her ten-year-old daughter, Suradhuni, were spending her days at her brother's house. The sudden death of her brother left them with no place to live. Narayani consulted with her husband, and with his approval, she sent people to bring them to her home. They arrived, and having arrived at her daughter's home, Digambari started not only to boss over her daughter but also over Ram. From the outset, she harbored strong dislike for Ram.

That morning, Ram brought a small sapling of peepul tree, and started planting it in the middle of their courtyard. Sitting at the verandah before the kitchen, Digambari counted her beads, and asked Ram in a shrill voice, "What are you doing, Ram?"

Ram looked at her. "The peepul tree shall give enough shade when it grows up. The teacher at school has said that the shade of the peepul is good for our health. Gobind, go, and bring a pot filled with water. Bhola, go cut a thick bamboo, we have to fence it, or else the cattle will eat it up."

Enraged beyond herself, Digambari muttered, "A peepul tree in the middle of the courtyard! Goodness me, never seen such queer happening in my father's lifetime!"

Ram had no ears for her remarks.

In the meantime, Gobind, in his limited capacity, brought a small pot of water. Smiling at him with adoration, Ram said, "Such negligible amount of water won't help, dear. You wait here, I shall go and fetch water."

After that, Ram poured several pails of water on the tree, muddying the entire courtyard. As he finished planting his sapling, Narayani returned after having her bath in the river. Digambari was burning in fire, for right before her eyes, the entire incident took place, from start to finish. As she saw her daughter entering, she screamed at the top of her voice. "Just see, Narayani, just have a look. He's planting a peepul tree in the middle of the courtyard. He says it will give shade. And look there, the rascal Bhola has cut a whole bamboo shrub because the plant needs to be fenced, he says!"

Narayani saw that indeed, Bhola dragged a pile of bamboo and bamboo sticks. Bhola was almost the same age as Ram. Watching their foolishness, Narayani fell into laughter. On one side, her mother seemed angry. On the other side, Ram's craziness and the whole affair seemed too ridiculous to her. Smiling, she asked, "What will you do with the peepul tree in the middle of the courtyard?"

Ram's surprise was visible for all to see. "What do you mean, *Boudi* (sister-in-law)? It will give us cool shade, and that branch high up there, when it grows, I shall hang a swing there for Gobind. Bhola, we must put the fence high up, or else kali, the cow will eat up the branches. Give me that axe, you won't be able to manage cutting it." And at once, he began chopping the bamboo, raising terrible noise.

Laughing in mirth, Narayani walked into the kitchen to put down the pitcher full of water that she had been carrying.

Digambari's eyes flashed in anger. She cast an irate look at her daughter and queried, "You said nothing, did you? Then let the peepul tree grow there!"

Smiling, Narayani said, "Ma, why are you getting worked up? Can such a big tree grow there? It has got no roots, just by pouring pails of water will not help it grow. It will dry down tomorrow."

Her words failed to calm down Digambari. "Dry down, my foot! If you wish for peace, just pull it up and uproot it soon."

Alarmed, Narayani replied, "No, no, then we'll all be doomed!"

Digambari went on. "Why? Is this house only his that he can plant the peepul tree as per his wishes? Isn't this house yours too? And isn't it also of my grandson, Gobind? Just to think that so many crows, kites, and vultures would make their nest on the branches of this tree. They would make the place filthy, dropping bones, Oh God! It won't be possible for me to stay here if that happens. Why are you people so afraid of him tell me?" she asked. "If this had been my home, Narayani, I would have fixed him in one day."

Narayani could visualize the inside of her mother's heart as clearly as a mirror. Falling silent for a while, she forced herself to smile. "He is just a kid, Ma. Would any wise person plant a peepul tree in the middle of one's own courtyard? After a couple of days, he'd himself throw it away."

Digambari replied, "Throw it away, you say? Well, why should he do that? I will throw it away myself."

"No Ma, don't do that," said Narayani. "You don't know him. Nobody would dare touch that thing other than me, not even his brother. Do nothing like that," she cautioned again.

That afternoon, Narayani was sewing the pillow cover in her room. Netya came rushing inside and informed her about the disaster. "Mistress, something terrible has happened. Grandma has uprooted the young master's plant. He will spare none of us when he returns from school today."

Dropping the sewing, Narayani rushed outside in a jiffy. She saw indeed the tree had disappeared!

She asked, "Ma, what has happened to Ram's tree?"

Pulling a long face, Digambari pointed out at the tree. "There it is!"

Coming closer, Narayani saw that the tree was not only uprooted, but its branches were also crushed and broken. In silence, she picked it up and threw it outside her home. Then she returned to her room.

On his return from school, Ram went to see his tree bubbling with enthusiasm, and jumped up in the air, when he saw the tree was gone. Throwing away his books and note copies, he screamed out, "*Boudi*, where is my tree?"

"Come here, I will explain."

When Ram came to her, holding his hand, she took him inside her room. She made him sit on her lap, and stroking his face and head, said, "Should you plant a peepul tree on a Tuesday?"

Calming down, Ram asked, "Why, what happens then?"

Smiling, Narayani replied, "Then, the eldest daughter-in-law of the family dies."

For a second, Ram turned pale. Then he said, "That's a lie."

"Check the almanac. See for yourself. It is written there," Narayani explained, with a smile.

"All right, show me the almanac, then."

Turning fearful, Narayani feigned surprise at once. "Oh, what kind of a boy you are! One shouldn't even mention the name of almanac on Tuesday- and you're asking to see it? Even Bhola knows about this. Call him, he'll tell you."

Afraid of his ignorance being caught up in Bhola's presence, Ram put his arms around the neck of his sister-in-law, who was indeed a mother figure in his life. Hiding his face there, he simply said, "Oh yes, I know that. But if we threw it away, then there comes no harm, isn't that so, *Boudi*?"

Pressing his head close to her, Narayani said, "No, then there is no harm." Her eyes moistened with tears. In a low voice, she asked, "What will you do if I die, Ram?"

Ram rocked his head. "No, one mustn't say things like that."

Drying her tears, Narayani said, "I'm aging, I must also die one day!"

Ram took it to be a joke. Lifting his head, he smiled and asked, "Oh really, are you old? You haven't lost a tooth, not one of your hairs has turned grey."

"Even before they turn grey, I shall one day drown myself in the river," she went on. "I shall leave for my bath, but shall not return."

"Why, *Boudi*?"

"Because of you. You can't stand my mother; you quarrel with her day and night. The day I don't return, you will all realize how it is."

Although Ram didn't believe her, but he felt fearful in his heart. "All right, I shall not behave like that anymore; but why is she always after me?"

"What if she does? She is my mother, she is your elder too, just as you love me, you must love her, too."

Ram again hid his face against her *aanchal*. It is in this manner that he had grown up with his sister-in-law, since the past thirteen years. How could he lie to her? It was impossible for him to think that.

Narayani's voice caught in her throat. "What's the point in hiding your face, Ram" she asked him in a gentle voice.

Just then, Digambari passed that way. In a honeyed voice, she said, "Seems like you have nothing better to do, Narayani. You're pampering your brother-in-law, while there, your own son is crying for you."

At once, Ram looked up. His eyes blazed like a ferocious wild animal. Narayani forced his face away from Digambari. "What has happened to my son?"

Digambari left from the place, as she could not cook up an instant lie. Ram lifted his head and said, "I'm going to strangle that witch!"

Putting her hand on his mouth, Narayani said, "Quiet, hush up. She is my mother."

Some days later, while having his meal, Ram gulped down a few sips of water, and then, flinging away the plate of rice, he stood up, prancing up and down. "I will not eat food cooked by that old witch, my mouth is blistering with fire... *Boudi, O Boudi...*"

His scream made Narayani rush out, leaving her daily prayers. "What happened, Ram?"

Full of anger, Ram cried. "I will not eat... not at all...."

Throw her away from home." Saying so, he rushed out of home in a jiffy.

Stupefied, Narayani stood in silence for a while. "Ma, so many times I've told you, don't put so much spice in the curry. People in this house dislike such spicy food," she told her mother.

Digambari flared up in anger. "What spicy you're talking about? I've just put a paste of two chilies. It isn't that spicy at all!"

Irked, Narayani countered, "You might as well not put two chilies, Ma. Why do that when no one can eat?"

"Oh, shut up, Narayani, just shut up! Are you now going to teach me how to cook? I've been doing this ever since. And now, my own daughter will teach me to cook, fie on me!"

Spreading her legs at the doorstep, Digambari sat and beat her forehead. Crying in a high-pitched voice, she exclaimed, "Oh my brother, where did you go, leaving me? Call me there, too. I can't bear this anymore. He abuses me with filthy words! I'm a witch, I'm an old hag! He asks me to be thrown away from this house! Oh, why am I eating food at my daughter and son-in-law's home! Let me hang myself! It is a hundred times better to beg on the roads! Suro, come dear, let's leave this house. I'm not going to drink a drop of water in this house."

Almost on the verge of tears, Suro came and waited near her mother. Digambari held her hand and left.

Keeping the *boti* (a curved blade rising out of a narrow, wooden base) aside, Narayani got up, walked up to her mother, and stopped her.

Shedding copious tears, Digambari said, "No, don't stop us, Narayani, let us go. We shall die in starvation under a tree, but we shall not accept your food, shall not sleep here again."

Folding her hands, Narayani said, "Whom are you angry with, Ma, that you are leaving us? Have we erred in any way?"

Digambari's wail increased. In a nasal accent, she lamented, "Am I a silly girl not to see through the reality? I understand well that without your approval, he'd never have the guts to disrespect me. I'm a witch, a hag, I must me thrown away, isn't that what he said? All right, let us go away then. We are just a burden on you all. Leave my way, Narayani, let me go."

Touching her mother's feet, Narayani pleaded. "Forgive us for today. Let my husband come, then do as you wish." Then holding her mother's hand, she took her inside, washed her feet with water, dried it with her *aanchal*, and made her sit on a *pinri* (a raised wooden platform to sit) and waved the fan for her.

For the moment, it calmed Digambari down. But in the afternoon, as Shyamlal sat down to have his meal, she whimpered and cried from behind the door in the kitchen. Flabbergasted, at first, Shyamlal could understand none of it. Later, as he grasped the incident, he got up without finishing his meal. Narayani understood the cause of his anger.

Nrityakali, the outspoken one in the house, was quick to comment. "Grandma made a scene intentionally, and did not let the master eat in peace. Were the tears in your eyes drying up? You could have shed them after he had eaten."

With an ashen face, Digambari kept quiet.

In the afternoon, Ram returned home. Having searched everywhere, he came to his sister-in-law's room and saw that she was sleeping with Gobind. He sensed that something was not right. Yet, he said, slowly, "I'm feeling hungry."

His sister-in-law did not answer. Raising his voice, he asked, "What shall I eat?"

Still sleeping, Narayani replied, "I don't know. Go away from here."

"No, I won't, I'm feeling hungry, I said."

Turning her face away, in an angry voice Narayani said, "Don't pester me, Ram. Netya is there, ask her."

Without further words, Ram searched for Netya, and asked her to give some food.

Netya was, perhaps, ready. She at once brought out a bowl of milk, some puffed rice, and a few coconut sweets. Angered, Ram asked, "Only this?"

Netya replied, "Young master, don't cause a ruckus today if you wish well. Master has left for his office without finishing his meal. And the mistress too has eaten nothing, she's gone to sleep with Gobind. If she hears the commotion now, and comes here- then you're in for big trouble, I can assure you of that!"

Ram had already witnessed some part of it, so without further ado, he drank the milk and filling the lap of his loincloth with the puffed rice and the coconut sweets, he went out beside the pond, and sat there. He had lost all appetite. His sister-in-law was hungry. Absent-mindedly, he chewed the puffed rice, and thought if only he knew a mantra like those sages, he'd have been able to make his sister-in-law eat from afar. But without knowing the mantra, he wasn't certain how to do this. The thought of going back home and entreating her to eat brought a sense of shame over him. Besides, his brother too had not taken his meal. She wouldn't pay any heed to my pleadings, Ram thought. Pouring the puffed rice on the pond, he wandered away from there. Each time he thought his *Boudi* was starving, a needle seemed to prick in his heart.

At night, Shyamlal told his wife, "This is now becoming unbearable to me. It is impossible to live with him."

Surprised, Narayani asked, "Whom are you talking about?"

"About Ram, of course. Your mother has been telling me since four-five days about how Ram insults her for no reason. I'm going to call five gentlemen from this village, and keeping them as witness, I am going to divide the landed property. Let him stay apart from us. I can't handle this anymore."

Stunned, Narayani sat in silence for a while. "You're going to separate Ram from us?" she asked. "Don't even say that. He's an infant, immature and young, what would he do with the landed property?"

"Yeah, an infant, indeed," mocked Shyamlal. "It is not my business to think what he would do with his share of the landed property."

Narayani replied, "He knows nothing, I know. So, has my mother been telling you all this for the past days?"

Embarrassed, Shyamlal hesitated. "No, not that she has been complaining. But I have eyes too, do you think I have noticed nothing?"

"No, I didn't mean that," she replied. "But he has no one, with whom is he going to live, separated from us? He has no mother, no sister, not even an aunt. Who is going to cook for him?"

Irritated, Shyamlal replied, "How do I know that!"

But although he said that, in his heart Shyamlal understood the situation only too well. How would he evade such a glaring truth?

Controlling herself, her voice thick with emotion, Narayani said, "See, at thirteen, when girls dabble with their dolls, then your mother entrusted the running of this household most comfortably to me, and went to heaven. She must be watching me now if I've been able to carry this household forward. I've cooked and fed, brought up my son, fulfilled my social duties, my duties towards the relatives, everything I've carried on my head, as I turned to be a woman of twenty-six. Now, if you come and meddle with me and my household affairs, I promise I shall drown myself in the river. Then you may remarry, separate Ram, and continue with your life as per your wish. I shall not comment. But no, not now."

Shyamlal feared his wife; he uttered no more words. The conversation stopped there for that night. The next day, Narayani called Ram, made him sit near her, and stroking his back with great tenderness, she said, "Ram, it is better that you stayed elsewhere. Wouldn't you be able to live?"

At once, Ram agreed, and grinning said, "Oh, yes, I can do that, *Boudi*! You, me, Gobind, and Bhola. When shall we leave, *Boudi*?"

It rendered Narayani silent, what could she say? But Ram did not let the conversation end. He prodded. "*Boudi*, when can we go?"

In answer, she pulled him close to her, and said, "Wouldn't you be able to live without your *Boudi*?"

Ram shook his head. "No."

"And if *Boudi* dies?"

"Don't talk like that."

"You don't listen to me."

Ram protested at once. "When do I not listen to you?"

"When do you listen, tell me?" she asked. "I've told you so many times not to insult my mother, but you never spare a chance to do just that. Yesterday too you did the same. One day, I'll leave this house and go away wherever my two eyes take me."

"I'll come along."

"How would you know when I'd leave? I'll go away secretly."

"And Gobind?"

"He shall stay with you; you shall raise him up."

"I won't be able to do that, *Boudi*."

Narayani smile. "You have to."

Disbelieving her words, Ram now laughed out aloud. "This is all a joke. You will not go away anywhere."

"No, it is not a lie. I'll go away, you will see."

Regretting, Ram asked, "And if I listen to everything that you say?"

"Then I won't go away," Narayani said with a smile. "And you don't have to raise Gobind then."

Happy, Ram said, "All right, you watch from today."

3

Eight days passed in peace. Digambari continued to insinuate and remark, but Ram did not become angry. Although he did not believe in his *Boudi's* dire words completely, but he felt afraid. However, it seemed that God was ill-disposed with them, and an accident occurred soon.

Digambari had pledged to feed twelve brahmins to commemorate her late father's memory. She believed her father's ghost was staying in his son's house, but now it seemed to frequent her daughter's home- albeit in her dreams. To appease the ghost, that day, she decided to invite the twelve brahmins.

In the morning, while Ram was practicing Maths, Bhola entered quietly and reported, "Young master, come and see, *Bhaga Bagdi* has brought a net to capture your Kartik and Ganesh."

The fact was two ancient *Rui* fishes (Indian carp) floated in and out near the steps of the pond. They swam in the pond unafraid, and Ram, with love, had named them as Kartik-Ganesh. There was no one in the neighborhood who had not heard about the extraordinary description of their beauty and quality from Ram. Everyone had at least once paid a visit to them at his request. Only he knew their special abilities. And he was the only one who could distinguish between Kartik and Ganesh. Even Bhola sometimes made a mistake in recognizing them, and Ram soundly boxed his ears on such occasions!

Narayani would smile, and say, "After my death, Ram's Kartik and Ganesh would be put to use. (to feed the brahmins with fish as per cremation ritual)

Bhola's information did not bother Ram at all. Bending down on his slate, he said, "Let him try! They would tear his net and escape."

Bhola said, "No, young master, Bhaga has brought those strong nets used by the fishermen, that will not break or tear."

Keeping the slate aside, Ram said, "All right, let's have a look."

Reaching the pond, he witnessed the conspiracy being hatched against his Kartik-Ganesh.

Bhaga had sprinkled some puffed rice over the water and was poised to catch the fishes with his net.

Coming closer, Ram gave him a push. "You wretch, are you calling my fishes by giving them puffed rice?"

Almost on the verge of tears, Bhaga replied, "The master has ordered. We could not procure any other fish, young master."

Snatching the net from his hand, Ram threw it away. "Get lost, now."

Bhaga went away.

Coming back, Ram again sat down with his slate and pencil. He had promised not to upset anyone.

That day, Digambari was busy finishing her morning prayers. Netya came and informed, "Grandma, fishes were not available. Young master has sent away Bhaga after thrashing him."

Digambari had her greedy eyes upon these two fishes for long. Of course, she was a widow, one must not try to gauge how earnestly she desired the carp fishes! The fact was, she did not wish to have it for herself, but she wished in earnest to prepare a delicious fish dish and feed the good brahmins, and earn good merits and fame. The previous night she discussed with Shyamlal, and without mentioning about Kartik-Ganesh, she had loaned the thick net of the fishermen. Then, paying a small bribe to their tenant Bhaga bagdi, she had almost made sure to get those two fishes. That morning, having seen those fishes floating near the steps of the pond, she had sat down to repeat the name of her deity, counting the beads, feeling blissful. Being in this state, when she received the news, it made her lose the power to ascertain the good from the bad. Gnashing her teeth, and raising the bead strings, she exclaimed, "What an enemy I have! My bones shall feel light the day the rascal dies! I've not even broken my fast, if there is a God above, may He take him away within this night!"

Sitting close by, Narayani was chopping the vegetables. In a lightning speed, she stood up, and shouted loudly. "Ma!"

A call from the child addressing one's mother is second to none, they say. That day, the way Narayani addressed her mother was incomparable to any other call. That one call from her made the blood in Digambari's heart freeze. Narayani too could utter no more words. Tears streamed down her cheeks. Then, drying her eyes, she walked to the place where Ram was studying.

In a harsh voice she asked, "Have you thrashed Bhaga Bagdi and sent him away?"

Alarmed, Ram looked up from his slate, and looking at her face for a moment, he rushed out of the room, without attempting to give any reply to her.

As a result, Narayani could not know the truth behind the incident. Coming back, she sent for Bhaga and once again ordered him to fetch the fishes.

Bhaga went away and soon returned carrying a huge Rui fish on his shoulder. As he dashed the fish on the courtyard, from her kitchen door Narayani saw it.

Shaken and afraid, she asked, "Oh, have you, by any chance, caught the fish from the fishpond? Is this Ram's Kartik-Ganesh?"

Elated to have caught such an enormous fish, Bhaga exclaimed with glee. "Sure it is, mistress. This one is from the pond- a magnificent fish!" Then pointing his finger at Digambari, he informed, "The lady had instructed me to catch this one only."

Stupefied, Narayani stood motionless. Nrityakali who although was not so favorably disposed towards Ram, now was rather angry to look at the fish. "Grandma, everyone in the neighborhood knows the young master's fascination for these two fishes. Why did you ask to catch them? There are other ponds too, was there no fishes in them? Why do you need a fish weighing eighteen kilos to feed only ten people? Quick, hide this, he will be back soon."

Pulling a long face, Digambari said, "I don't know all that. It is just a fish, and just see what these people are up to! If you hide this, how shall I cook it and feed the brahmins?"

"Your brahmins are coming to eat only around two or half-past two in the noon," Netya replied. "There's still a lot of time. Let the young master first leave for his school, or else he will spare no one today. Oh, where did Bhola leave? He was standing here all this while. Perhaps he has gone to inform him. Mistress, do something, please don't keep standing."

Bhaga had borrowed the net from the fishermen, hoping to receive a few cents from Narayani, as bonus. Now, as he saw the situation turn for the worse, he gave up his hopes, and left with the net.

Bhola knew where to find Ram when a situation arose. Running, he reached the guava grove in a jiffy. Ram was sitting on a branch, his feet dangling in the air. He was munching on a guava, when Bhola arrived, panting furiously. "Come and see, young master, they have killed your Kartik."

Pausing with his munching, Ram said, "That can't be."

"Oh yes, the mistress had ordered to catch it, it is still lying on the courtyard. Come and have a look."

Jumping down from the tree, Ram raced like a storm, and reached the courtyard in no time. Taken aback, he stood in the middle of the courtyard, and screamed, "Oh, this is my Ganesh! *Boudi,* you ordered to catch it." Saying so, he fell upon the ground, and like a goat sacrificed, threw his legs in the air. Digambari, too, perhaps had no doubt about the cogency and the indomitable depth of his sorrow.

Narayani tried hard to feed him at night, but Ram pushed her hands away, and after fasting for the whole day, only ate a few morsels of rice and left.

Standing apart, behind the door, Digambari said to Shyamlal, "Please coax Narayani to eat, she won't eat otherwise, she has eaten nothing since morning."

"Why?"

In the absence of tears, Digambari made her voice sound rather feeble, and said, "I'm so sorry, a thousand times sorry. How was I to know that catching a fish from the pond to feed the brahmins would lead to such profanation of the Bible!"

Unable to understand anything, Shyamlal asked Netya, "Netya, what has happened?"

"The fish that grandma got caught was young master's Ganesh," Netya replied from afar.

Startled, Shyamlal exclaimed, "You mean the one from Ram's Kartik-Ganesh?"

"Yes," replied Netya.

It needed no further explanation. Shyamlal envisaged the whole incident from there on. "Hasn't Ram eaten?"

Netya replied, "No."

"Then there's no point asking Narayani to eat," Shyamlal said. "If he hasn't eaten, I don't think she would eat, either."

Digambari went on. "Had I known that it would lead to such a scene, I would never have raised the topic of feeding the brahmins. I've no idea why Narayani herself ordered to catch that fish; I said nothing. But now it seems it is all my fault. Please send us away to somewhere else, son. I don't feel like staying here anymore." Taking a pause, she began again, now in a crying tone. "It is my sheer bad luck, or else why would my brother die? And why would I be forced to stay here, bearing all the insults? We're completely helpless, son- I request you, with folded hands, you must make a separate provision for us."

Shyamlal became worried, but he could neither accept nor refuse her words.

Standing behind the screen, Narayani felt ashamed to

see her mother's shameless duplicity. Going back to Ram's room, she knocked on the closed door. "Dear boy, open the door once, please."

Ram was awake, but he did not respond.

Narayani again called him. "Get up, open the door."

In a loud voice, he replied, "I won't. You all are my enemies."

"All right, so be it. But open the door."

"No, no, no- I will not open the door."

True to his words, he didn't open the door. Inside, Shyamlal heard everything. When his wife came inside, he said, "Either you find some solution to this. Else I'm going to go away somewhere. I can't tolerate this anymore."

Narayani fell into thinking, but she had no answer.

Two-three days later, when Ram's anger still did not subside, Narayani started getting angry and frustrated. One evening, when Ram had still not returned from school, Narayani felt alarmed, and sat fuming. Just then, after taking a dip in the river, after collecting the news of the world, wishing ill for Ram, and after predicting the possible worse consequences of her eldest daughter's immature wisdom, Digambari entered home. On the way, she had explained to the neighbors how close in age she was with her daughter, and how her hairs had greyed in her young age, and how influential she had been in her brother's family. While on her way, she came to hear of an incident that made her almost fly in the air and reach home in record time.

Setting her feet in the courtyard, she spoke up in a high-pitched voice, "Have you heard what your beloved brother-in-law has done, Narayani?"

Ashen with fear, she asked, "What has he done?"

"He has gone to jail," Digambari informed. "Suits him right! Never seen such a rascal in my seven lives."

Happiness seemed to brim over her face and eyes. Paying no heed to her, Narayani called Netya. "Netya, why hasn't Ram come home till now? Send Bhola, let him go and fetch him."

"But I just heard the incident," said Narayani.

Netya lingered there to hear the rest of the incident. Hastening her up, Narayani said, "What are you waiting for? Haven't you heard what I said?"

As Netya left with hurried steps, Digambari laced her voice with concern, said, "You know what happened, Narayani..."

"First change your wet clothes, Ma," Narayani cut her short. "Then you can say what happened." Saying so, Narayani left the place.

Surprised, Digambari muttered to herself, "Oh, just see her anger."

The inability to bring over such a dramatic incident with full vigor made her stomach bloat with discomfort.

The incident was something like this- the landlord's son studied in the village school. He got into an argument with Ram during the lunch break. The topic being rather complex, the argument ended not in solution but in a fight. The landlord's son had claimed that the Scriptures had proclaimed *Shmashana Kali* (a ferocious form of the Goddess Kali in Hinduism) to be more watchful and potent than *Raksha Kali* (Kali in her protectress form) as her tongue sticks out longer.

Ram had protested saying that *Shmashana Kali's* tongue was broad, but not as long or as red as *Raksha Kali*. When the landlord's son refused to listen to him, and insisted that *Raksha Kali's* tongue was indeed rather small, it angered Ram.

"No, her tongue is long, and protruding. She protects

the world; hence we call her *Raksha Kali*, Kali the protectress. How can she protect this entire world if she had such a tiny tongue?"

One word led to another, and then to fist fighting. The landlord's son was not strong, so he got beaten up. Drops of blood oozed out of his nose. Such a huge incident had never occurred in the history of the tiny school. It was the landlord's school, and his son suffered a bloody nose! Closing the school, the headmaster accompanied the boy and left in search of justice. Needless to say, Ram had disappeared from the scene long before.

Returning, Bhola informed Ram was missing. A little later, Shyamlal came home, looking rather put out. Standing on the courtyard, he called out to his wife. "Are you listening? It seems like we must leave this village. I was earning a little and bringing home some money. Now, perhaps, that would stop soon, too."

Narayani came out from the storeroom, and standing at the doorstep asked in a dry voice, "Have they gone to the police station?"

Shaking his head, Shyamlal said, "The landlord has a golden heart, a godlike person, he has forgiven us, but there are others in the community. But if each day a new incident takes place, wouldn't it be difficult to stay in this village? Where is Ram?"

Narayani said that he had not returned yet. Perhaps, he had absconded in fear.

Turning serious, Shyamlal said, "Absconding or not, I've decided to sever all my ties with him. He's my stepbrother, I tolerated him lest others would cast aspersions, but not anymore. Now I must save myself first."

From the courtyard in front of the kitchen, Digambari added, "Yes, you must also think about your own son."

Delighted, Shyamlal answered, "Yes Mother, of course! Tomorrow I shall call five gentlemen from our community and shall divide the landed property. And listen, I'm telling you too Narayani, no need to scold him further about this. Let him do whatever he thinks fit. He thought it fit to raise his hand on my master's son, what can we do?"

Feeling rapturous in her heart, Digambari said, "I'm at a loss to understand why Narayani even tries to reprimand him, my heart trembles to see that. He's so stubborn, if he can insult me, would it be impossible for him to humiliate her too? Listen to my words, your self-esteem and your home comes first, don't bother about Ram."

Shyamlal had trouble in agreeing with these last words of his mother-in-law, perhaps his scruples were raised. He said, "Whatever it is, there is no need to discipline him anymore."

Like an image carved in stone, Narayani stood and heard every bit of that conversation. She did not utter a word, and slumped her way to work.

An hour later, Netya arrived, and said, "Mistress, the young master has come home."
Narayani got up without speaking and going into Ram's room, she bolted the doors from inside. Sitting on his bed, Ram was unaware, wrapped in his own thoughts. The sound of the doors closing startled him. He saw Boudi had closed the door, and she had picked up the thin bamboo cane from the corner of the room. He jumped to the other side of the bed. Narayani said, "Come here."

Folding his palms together, Ram said, "I shall never do it again, please forgive me this one time."

Like a hard taskmaster, Narayani said, "I'll cane you less if you come closer. Or else I shall break this cane on your body."

Yet, Ram did not budge from the place. Rooted in the same spot, he pleaded with her. "I'm giving you my promise, I will not do it again, I'm pulling my own ears."

Bending over the bed, Narayani hit him hard on his shoulders with the cane. And then the blows kept coming like showers. At first, he tried to escape, opening the side door; then, running around in the room, he tried to defend himself, and at last, he held her feet, crying out aloud to be spared. Netya who was observing everything from the window, cried out and said, "Mistress, spare him, I'm apologizing on his behalf..."

"Why do you always interfere in every matter," grimaced Digambari, making a face at Netya.

From his room, Shyamlal called out. "What's this? Are you going to cane him the entire night?"

Dropping the cane, Narayani said to Ram, "Remember this."

4

Ram was having his meal. Sitting further away, Digambari's voice rang out. "I don't understand. What was the need to cane such a big boy? His brother never scolds or beats him."

"You're the height, grandma," said Netya, as she went with her chores. "You're the one who complain everything to the mistress."

Ram had not enjoyed being caned that other night. Now, listening to Netya's words, he rolled his eyes and said, "The witch! She is going to gobble us all."

Digambari shouted out, complaining, "Narayani, listen to what your brother-in-law is saying."

Narayani was going for her bath. She replied in a tired voice, "I've no energy to listen anymore, Ma. I'm telling you honestly, Netya, I'll find peace only after my death. I can't take this anymore. You monkey, the scars on your back are still fresh. Have you forgotten everything so soon?"

Ram did not answer, and continued to eat. Narayani left to take her bath. In the courtyard, there was a guava tree. After having his meal, Ram climbed on the tree, and munched at random both the ripe and the unripe guavas. Some he ate fully, a few others he only nibbled and threw around. And the ones which were unripe, those he threw around in a careless manner. Watching that brought a burning sensation of anger over Digambari. Narayani was not around. She said, "Because of you, we can't bite a single ripe guava. Why are now wasting these unripe ones?"

Ram could not tolerate her, especially not after he heard from Netya that it was because of Digambari that Narayani had thrashed him. Seething in anger, he shouted from the top of the tree, "I'll do it again, you old hag!"

Of all the adjectives, this was the one Digambari detested the most. Distorting her face, she said, "Old Hag? Ok, let Narayani come. As is the evil, so must be its remedy. What a shameless boy! Despite the thrashing, he has no shame!"

From the tree, Ram said, "Old witch!"

"Old witch? What an audacious utterance! You scoundrel, you wretch, get down from there!"

Ram asked, "Why should I come down? Is it your father's tree?"

Furious, Digambari cried out, "What, you're abusing me? Did you hear that, Netya?"

Just then, Narayani returned from the river bath. One glance at the tree, and she said, "Why didn't you go to school after eating? Why are you there, up on that tree?"

Ram had planned to escape from the tree as he saw his

sister-in-law return, but being involved in the argument, he failed to see her return from the ghats. Now she stood right in the middle of the courtyard. In a casual voice, he said, "I'm having a guava."

"All right- but why didn't you go to school?"

"I'm having a stomach pain."

Enraged, Narayani asked, "Oh, that is why you're munching on an unripe guava after finishing your meal?"

Hearing her daughter's voice, Digambari rushed out. "The wretched boy, he takes my father's name and insults me. He said, why should I climb from the tree? Is it your father's tree?"

Raising her eyes, Narayani asked, "Did you say that?"

Frowning, Ram said, "No Boudi, I did not."

Digambari screamed out, "You didn't, you wretched creature? Netya is my witness." Then distorting her face, she mimicked in a nasal voice. "The other day when you're being thrashed, what did you say? Forgive me Boudi, I hold your two feet Boudi, the moment you get your freedom, you jump, you rascal!"

Ram could not tolerate any more. In his hand, he had a big, unripe guava. He threw it with force; it did not touch Digambari, but hit above Narayani's left eyebrow. For a moment, everything around her darkened, and she fell. Digambari screamed, Netya came rushing, dropping her work, and catching his breath, Ram ran out from there.

At noon, when Shyamlal came to have his bath and lunch, he saw Narayani was lying lifeless on the bed. Her right eye had swollen immensely, covering her eye. Netya was applying a wet compress and fanning her. That day, Digambari stood in front of her son-in-law, and cried out to him, "Ram has killed Narayani."

Startled, Shyamlal walked up to his wife. He examined

the wound himself, and in a hard voice, he said, "I swear upon you, from today if you give him food to eat, if you ever talk to him, if you involve yourself in anything related to him, then that day you may lose me."

Shaken up, Narayani said, "No, no, keep quiet, never utter such words."

"If you don't honor the oath I have taken, may you see me die on that very day." Saying so he went out to fetch the doctor.

Ram spent the whole day walking aimlessly beside the river, and thinking about the impossible scenarios. As evening descended, he crept inside home in darkness, unseen by anyone. At home, he saw they had erected a fence through the middle of the courtyard, dividing the house into two segments. Shaking the fence, he found it to be quite tough, and not to be broken. Peeping quietly in the kitchen, he saw the same arrangement there, too. A pile of brass utensils lay on the floor. Although he yet could not understand the true meaning of all this, something told him it must have some connection with the incident in the morning. His heart came to his mouth. Going back to his room, he sat quietly, trying to pick up the sounds coming from the other part of the house. Around nine o'clock, feeling hungry, he knocked on the back door. Netya opened it and stood away. "Where is Boudi?" Ram asked.

"Sleeping in her room."

Inside, he saw Boudi was lying on the bed, while Digambari sat on the mat on the floor, with her younger daughter. Gobind was playing. Watching Ram, he came running to him, and pulling his hand, he said, "Uncle, your house is on the other side, our house is on this side. Father has said that if you come our way, he'll break your legs."

As Ram sat near the foot of Narayani on the bed, she

folded her feet away. He sat in silence. Leaning against her young daughter, Digambari prodded her. "Suro, tell him what your brother-in-law has told us."

Suradhuni blabbered out in a rush. "Brother in-law has asked you not to come here. Tomorrow morning—"

Digambari prompted her daughter, "the landed property."

Suradhuni continued. "Tomorrow morning, he shall divide the landed property."

Digambari again prompted, "Tell him about the oath, you affected girl!"

"Brother in-law has made Didi swear she wouldn't serve you food anymore, wouldn't talk to you...."

Narayani scolded her sister from the bedside. "Enough, now stop."

Then Digambari took over. "What to do? You almost half killed her. Would your brother not force her to take such an oath? I can't blame him at all. It will not be possible for you to come to this house, have food here. She must adhere to her husband's words."

A suppressed wail seemed to rise in Ram's breast. And yet, remembering Digambari's grimace in the morning, he couldn't for once ask forgiveness from his Boudi. He could not cry out, and say '*I shall not do it again, Boudi!*' These words had protected him several times in the past, but tonight the words did not come, and the helpless feeling suffocated him.

Then, in a tired voice, Narayani said, "Suro, ask him to leave."

Stifling out his sobs, he said, "Ask him to leave! Am I not hungry? I've eaten such a long time ago."

Agitated, Narayani said, "Why couldn't he finish me completely? Then he could have feasted. I don't know- ask him to go to Netya."

"No, I won't go anywhere. I'll fast and go to bed." Saying these words, Ram walked away with noisy footsteps and went to his own room. When Netya brought him some food, he shouted at her. "Get lost, accursed one!"

Netya left the food there and went away. Ram dashed the utensils in the courtyard in anger.

In the morning, after Shyamlal left for his work, Ram walked on his part of the courtyard and he muttered aloud, "I don't care for such oaths. Who is he to give oaths? He is not my brother; I don't care about his words. Have I hit him? I wanted to hit only the old hag, it has hurt only Boudi, why are they making her swear?"

No one from the other side responded. Then, changing his tone, he said, "All right, it is fine if no one talks to me, no one gives me food to eat. I'll cook for myself; it will be fun- Rice, lentils, yummy vegetables, fish- I'll have a sumptuous meal alone. It won't matter to me."

No one responded to these words either from the other side. Then, walking inside his kitchen, he worked, making noises with his utensils. Calling Bhola, he commanded him to wash the rice and lentils, and chop the vegetables. Netya brought all the items into his kitchen. Ram then told Bhola, "You're my servant, don't go to their home. And if anyone from their side comes here, then break their legs-let Netya come once on this side!"

Sitting on her side of the courtyard, Narayani listened in silence. Curious, her mother peeped through the fence, and soon she came up to her eldest daughter and whispered to her, "Oh, just see the wisdom of the boy! He has filled the bronze vessel up to its rim with rice and added only a handful of water. Just to feed one, he is cooking for ten people! And how will the rice cook, pray? It is going to burn into charcoal. Neither the vessel can hold so much rice, nor such a little water can boil it. And then, he boasts about his culinary expertise! I cook so well, but never boast about it. He should compete with me, let people decide whose cooking is the best!"

Narayani turned her face away.

"Grandma is too much," commented Netya. "The young master has never taken a glass of water himself. How can he cook today?" She was an old maid in the family, and she found the situation not to her liking.

Following her mother, Surodhuni too was peeping through the fence. An hour later, she came running to her elder sister and pulled her arm. "Didi, come and see, Ram dada is eating the uncooked rice. Good heavens! Didi, won't he have a stomachache if he eats such uncooked food?"

Pushing away her arm, Narayani got up and laid down on her bed. She understood only too well how intense his hunger was that goaded him to eat those uncooked morsels of rice!

At noon, after Shyamlal finished his meal, Digambari called her daughter. "Have some food, Narayani. You have a slight temperature running, but you could still have some food. It won't harm you."

Covering herself with the thick blanket, Narayani went to sleep. "Don't irritate me, Ma. You all have food."

"Shall I make you two flat breads, instead of rice?"

"No, I want nothing."

Surprised, Digambari asked, "What kind of response is that? You're fasting since yesterday; you must eat a few morsels today."

There came no response from Narayani.

Netya replied, "You're wasting your breath for no reason, grandma. Even if you stand the whole day and blabber, you won't make the mistress eat. She's running a fever, let her rest."

In the evening, Narayani came and sat on the verandah facing the kitchen. Each time her eyes met Netya, she wished to say something, but could not.

Coming home from school, Ram bought puffed rice and molasses from the shop. While eating, he raised his voice and said, "Did anything happen to me? I ate rice, and I went to school, and now again I'm eating. I am fine."

He understood everyone was present on the other side of the fence, but just as in the morning, no one responded. It made him restless. Shouting, he said, "This is my side, my boundary. If Netya, or anyone else, comes this way ever, I'll break their legs."

He had already voiced the threat of ⊚breaking the leg', but it had yielded nothing then. Now too, it went in vain. Worse, it wasn't clear if it scared anyone! In the evening, switching on the light, he went inside the kitchen and started shouting again. "Where are my woods? How will I cook? Where are my mortar and pestle? How will I prepare the spice paste?"

From the other side of the fence, Netya replied, "The mistress will get you a new mortar and pestle tomorrow."

"No, I don't want that." Saying so, he went out of the kitchen and cried.

He returned soon and started firing questions to the other side. "Why did you all kill my Ganesh? Why did the old witch tease me like that in her nasal accent? It is just right that I abused her- may she be born as a hag in her next birth!"

Angered, Digambari rolled her eyes. "Did you listen, Narayani? Isn't he provoking a fight with no reason?"

Narayani continued staring far away. She spoke nothing.

5

From next day morning, there came a change in Ram's conversation. Two days had gone by, Boudi had not called him, nor served him food. It had never happened before in his life. It frightened him. At first, he offered meaningless explanations. Once he said he had thrown the guava to hit the cat, then he said he had just wanted to throw the unripe guava away. Then again, he said, he abused no one. Later, he explained he was abusing Gobind; no, he was in fact intending to abuse Bhola. But no matter what he said, nothing worked. No one from the other side made any response. Then, with a lot of difficulty, summoning up courage and shedding shame, he said that he would never do that again, but that confession too went unheard. Nobody spoke up from the other side of the fence.

Then he quietly cried. How was he going to make Boudi happy? Boudi had separated him to stay alone. Where would he go then? With whom and how would he live? He could find no clue. That day, he did not cook, he did not go to school, he just lay on his bed.

Perhaps, because of shedding tears in secret, Narayani had a fever the night before. She drank a few sips of milk when her mother brought the bowl to her, but then put the bowl down. She felt it humiliating to argue with her mother.

Around nine o'clock, Netya came in, and whispered, "Mistress, it is rather late at night, but there's no sound from the young master's home."

Restless, Narayani sat up on her bed and fell into crying. "My dear one, Netya, see if he's at home."

Netya's eyes turned wet, too. Drying her eyes with her hand, she said, "I'm afraid to go there, mistress." Later, when Bhola informed Ram was indeed in his room, and was sleeping, Narayani folded her hands and thanked the Gods for keeping him safe.

The next morning, before it was dawn, she finished her bath and made the preparation to cook. Halfway through her cooking, Digambari came and was stunned to see her daughter in the kitchen. "You're running a fever, isn't it, Narayani? For the last three days, you have not eaten. You took a bath early in the morning. What are you doing like this?"

In a normal, slow voice, Narayani replied, "I'm cooking, as you can see."

"I can see. But why? Won't you eat the food cooked by me?"

Narayani did not answer.

Since the whole day, Ram had wondered how much pain Boudi must have endured! Taking an unripe guava, he had been hitting his forehead to estimate the intensity of pain his sister-in-law must have felt. At last, he wondered what he could do to erase this wrongful act. Thinking he remembered that sometime ago his Boudi had asked him to live somewhere else, away from this house. In the end, he decided that if he went away to some other place, it might bring happiness to her. His maternal grandparents lived somewhere near *Tarakeshwar* (A small town in Hoogly district in West Bangal), but he had no proper idea of it. He thought he would look them up once reaching there. He prepared a small bundle and waited for the dawn to break.

Narayani finished her cooking. She was arranging the cooked items neatly on a plate. Near the door, Bhola came and called her. "What is it, Bhola?" she asked.

For these past days, Bhola had looked after the cows, but he had not entered the house, fearing Ram. He whispered now, "I have something to say in secret."

When Narayani came closer, he whispered again. "Whatever you had said, the young master will do that, only if you spare two rupees."

Unable to understand, she asked, "What will he do, dear? To whom I must pay?"

A bit surprised, Bhola said, "You had asked him to go away, right? He's agreed to go away. All right, give me one rupee, if you can't spare two."

Worried, Narayani asked, "Where has he agreed to go? Where is he?"

"He's standing under the tree outside," Bhola informed. "He is leaving for his maternal grandparents' house."

"Go, and call him soon, tell him, I am calling him."

Bhola ran out, as Narayani stood watching. A little later, Ram walked in, carrying his small bundle. Narayani held his hand and took him inside.

From afar, Digambari, with a sinking feeling in her heart, watched Ram entering the kitchen. As she walked inside, she saw Ram sitting on Narayani's lap, before the well-arranged plate of food, while Narayani's tears fell on his back, on his head, like the shower of rains. Stunned, Digambari stared at the scene for a while, and then said, "Oh, is that why you were busy cooking? You're going to serve food to him? And the oath that my son-in-law made you take, is it of no worth to you, then?"

Raising her head, Narayani replied, "Why should it be worthless, Ma? I did not disregard his oath. I did not eat for three days, and I didn't serve Ram food for three days."

In a sharp tone, Digambari said, "Really? Is this not disregarding his words? Have you taken his permission?"

Tolerating a deep blow, Narayani said, her voice rather curt. "Yes, I have."

Digambari did not believe her. More agitated, she

said, "You think I'm a small baby? Would I not have known if you had asked for your husband's permission?"

It was now impossible for Narayani to bear any further. Turning harsher, she replied, "How would you know when and from whom I got the permission? Anyone can talk, can swear, and pass on the oath, but—" and she now forcibly lifted Ram's abashed face, and kissed on his forehead- "but the one who has brought up a small baby, and raised him for years, only that person knows where the oath must stop. Please do not bother about this, Ma. Now, leave this place. Let me help him eat a few morsels. The kid has not eaten for three days." And while saying so, her eyes started shedding copious tears again.

"Would I then be able to stay here?" After a moment's pause, Digambari asked. "I'm telling your clearly today, I shall not be able to stay here anymore."

Narayani replied, "I was also hesitating to bring up this topic, Ma. You're right, it shall not be possible for you to stay here. My grown-up child has shriveled up before your eyes. He might be mischievous, but in my home, before my eyes, I shall allow no one to punish him like that. You may stay for today, but please leave for your home tomorrow. I shall send your costs, but you cannot stay here anymore."

Digambari turned stiffly, and then slowly walked out from there. Ram slowly said, "No Boudi, let her stay. I've now gained wisdom; I've turned better now. Give me one more chance."

Looking at him through the tears in her eyes, Narayani kissed his forehead again. "First finish your meal."

Munshi Premchand

The Salt Inspector
Namak ka daroga

1

A new department was set up. It banned the trade of salt-
a gift from God. As a result, people traded it illegally,
devising various kinds of nefarious means. Some started
offering bribes, while others resorted to underhand tactics.
They welcomed it as a stroke of good luck. The officials
started giving up their honorable posts and preferred
joining this department. Even the lawyers longed to be
appointed to the post of salt inspector.

People in those days identified English education as
Christianity. In their minds, both were interchangeable.
Persian was still the dominant language. People fluent in
Persian were easily appointed to the highest positions.
Munshi Vanshidhar was no exception to this rule. Having
finished reading the tale of Zulaikha, he decided that the
story of *Siri and Farhad* (A classic Persian story) was a much
elevated one, compared to the tale of *Nal and Neel* (The
two monkeys in the epic Ramayana who are credited as
the builder of the bridge across the ocean), and even to the
narrative about America's discovery. He searched for a job.

His father was an experienced man. He advised him. "Son! The family's penury is quite visible to you. We're under the burden of debt. The girls in the family are growing up fast, like weeds. I'm like a tree likely to collapse at any moment. You're now the master of this house. At a job, your post and position are like the mausoleum of a sage. Your focus should always be on the extra offerings that come along. Please find a job that guarantees such 'extra' earnings, on top of your salary. Salary is the full moon, visible for a day, then it wanes and decreases; but the 'extra' earnings, on top of your salary, are like a running stream that quenches man's thirst. Man gives salary, hence, it doesn't grow as much; but God decrees the 'extra' earning, hence it makes people prosperous. But then, you're an intelligent person. You don't need explanation. Let your conscience guide you on this path. Look at people, try to judge their needs, then proceed. One should be rather harsh with people who seek favors from you. However, it is always tough to break the ones who didn't need any favors. These words arise from the core of my experiences. Please keep them in mind."

The father then blessed Vanshidhar after this discourse. He was an obedient son, and he set off from home, having listened attentively to his father's words. In this vast world, endurance was his ally, knowledge was his guide, and self-sufficiency was his biggest support. He had an auspicious start, and soon he adorned the post of the salt inspector. He would receive a good salary coupled with the opportunity to make 'extra' earnings. When his old father heard the good news, his happiness knew no bounds. His creditors turned easy, and the revival of good times was in the air. Only the neighbors felt jealousy prick their hearts.

2

On that freezing, winter night, the soldiers and the guards at the Salt Department slept in a drunken stupor. It was only six months that Munshi Vanshidhar took the post of a salt inspector. But during this short duration, he had impressed the higher authorities with his expertise and his decent behavior. The officers trusted him immensely. Almost a mile away from his department, the river *Yamuna* (The second-largest tributary river of the Ganges) flowed past. Over the river stood a boat bridge. The inspector was having a good sleep inside his closed room. But the sound of rattling carts and the noise of the boatmen roused him up from his sleep. Used to listening to the soft gurgling of the Yamuna, he now wondered why were the carts crossing the bridge at this late hour? Something was surely amiss here. He pensively reflected on it for a moment and braced himself with rising suspicion. Getting up, he put on his uniform, kept the pistol in his pocket, and riding on his horse, he quickly reached the riverbank. Watching the long queue of carts crossing the bridge, he asked annoyingly, "Whose carts are these?"

For a moment, silence ensued. The men whispered amongst themselves, and then replied saying, "These belong to pandit Alopidin."

"Who is he?"

"He's from the village Daataganj."

The name surprised Munshi Vanshidhar, because pandit Alopidin was one of the most well-known landlords of the area. His business ran into lakhs of rupees, and there was hardly any businessman in the area who wasn't indebted to him. He had a thriving business and was a competent entrepreneur. The British officers came for hunting in his village. He hosted them in his house and tended to their comfort for months.

Munshi Vanshidhar asked, "Where are these carts heading for?"

"Kanpur."

He wanted to know the contents inside the sacks; no one replied, and a deep silence spread around, heightening the inspector's doubts. Pausing for their response, he shouted out at them. "Have you all turned mute? Tell me, what's there inside these carts?"

When he received no response, he walked towards one of the carts and examined the content inside the cart. His suspicions were confirmed. Inside the cart, there were indeed chunks of salt.

3

Seated on his swanky-looking chariot, pandit Alopidin was on his journey with full ease. A few anxious cart drivers woke him up from his half-sleepy state. "Master, the inspector has stopped the carts, and he's summoned you to the riverside."

Pandit Alopidin's faith on goddess Lakshmi, the goddess of wealth, was deep. In his opinion, she ruled not only on earth but also in heaven. And his opinion seemed perfectly correct. After all, justice and law were mere toys in her hands; she manipulated them the way she wished. Not budging from his reclining state, he said, "You go. I'll be there. Quite nonplussed, he then leisurely made a *paan* (A preparation combining betel leaf with areca nut, widely used in Southeast Asia) for himself. Then wrapping himself with the quilt, he walked up to the inspector and said, "God bless you Sir! What is my mistake that you have stopped my carts? You should have some mercy for us Brahmins."

In a curt voice, Vanshidhar replied, "By the order of the Government."

Laughing, pandit Alopidin said, "For us, you're the government. We know neither the government nor their rules. Between us, it is like in a family. Am I not part of this cozy setup? You took needless troubles. I cannot cross this shore and forget to make an offering to the presiding lord of the shore. I was coming to meet you."

His words, laced with the tune of wealth, failed to impress Vanshidhar. He was new to his job, and the wave of honesty swelled high. His tone implacable, he said, "I'm not one of those treacherous people who'd sell their integrity in exchange for a few pennies. You are now under arrest. We will treat you as per the law. There is no time for more talks. Badlu Singh, please take him into custody. It is my order."

Pandit Alopidin was stupefied. Pandemonium broke out among the cart drivers. Such harsh words astonished pandit Alopidin. Badlu Singh took a step towards him, but could not muster enough courage to handcuff pandit Alopidin. Never had he seen righteousness make such a gross mockery of wealth. Alopidin reflected Vanshidhar was rather reckless because of his young age and was unimpressed by the power of wealth. He was too rash and reluctant. Pleading, he said, "Please don't do this, young sir. It is going to finish me. It shall tarnish my honor. What would you gain by disrespecting me? Don't treat me like a stranger, please."

His voice severe, Vanshidhar said, "I'm not willing to listen to such things."

The ground, which Alopidin thought to be rock solid, suddenly slipped away under his feet. His self-respect and his prosperity were hit badly. Yet, his faith in the numerical potency of wealth did not fully diminish. Turning to his assistant, he said, "Please offer one thousand rupees to the inspector. He's behaving just like a hungry lion now."

His words enraged Vanshidhar. "Not even a hundred thousand rupees would deter me from the path of honesty."

The meaningless stubbornness and the divine sacrifice presented by righteousness annoyed pandit Alopidin. Both the powers now engaged in a fight, and wealth now leaped higher, using its numerical power. Alopidin's offer reached from one to five, five to ten, ten to fifteen, and finally to twenty thousand rupees. But the spirit of uprightness put up a brave fight and stood alone, immovable like a mountain, against the huge numerical strength of wealth.

Disappointed, Alopidin said, "It is not in my power to offer you more. Please do whatever you like."

Vanshidhar called out to his subordinate. Cursing him silently, Badlu Singh took steps towards Alopidin. Afraid, the pandit stepped back. In a meek voice, he repeated, "Please have mercy on me, Sir. I'm ready to settle this issue for twenty-five thousand rupees."

"No, that is not possible."

"Thirty thousand rupees?"

"It is not possible."

"Even not for forty thousand?"

"Not even for four hundred thousand. Badlu Singh, please arrest this man. I will not hear a single word now."

Righteousness trampled upon wealth. Alopidin saw a powerful man walking towards him. In despair, he glanced around himself with hopeless eyes and then collapsed and fell.

4

The world slept, but its tongue wagged. As dawn broke forth, the whole town was abuzz with this news.

People remarked on pandit Alopidin's character. The world suddenly seemed devoid of all sins and sinners, except him. The milkman who sold milk diluted with water, the officer who filled his ledger with false entries, the clerks travelling without a ticket by trains, the moneylenders who made fraud dossiers- all shook their heads like gods.

The next day, when pandit Alopidin, accused, handcuffed, and in police presence, walked towards the courthouse, his head held down in shame, his heart brimming with anguish and anger, it perturbed the city immensely. It became so crowded that there remained no distinction between the wall and the roof.

But once he reached the courthouse, pandit Alopidin was like a lion in his own territory. There, the officials admired him, the staff worshipped him; the lawyers were his obedient servants, and orderlies, watchmen, and others worked willingly, like slaves, for him. All of them rushed to him the moment he stepped inside the court. Alopidin's act did not surprise them at all; it only surprised them to see him caught in the clutches of law. How could a wealthy person who talked so smoothly be nabbed in this manner? They all expressed their sympathy for him.

Promptly, a battery of lawyers was set up to counter this attack on him. On the battlefield of law, there now ensued a fight between righteousness and wealth. Vanshidhar waited in silence. Other than truth, he had no power and other than mere facts, he had no weapons in his arsenal. There were witnesses, but greed shook them immensely.

In fact, he realized that justice, too, seemed strained. The officers in that court of justice were drugged with partisanship. Justice and partisanship did not go together. If there was partisanship, how could one expect justice there? The case was soon over.

In his judgement, the Deputy Magistrate decreed: "All the evidence presented against pandit Alopidin was false and baseless. He is a man of reputation. It is beyond one's imagination to assume that he would break the law for such a small profit. Although the salt inspector Munshi Vanshidhar is not much to be blamed either, it is unfortunate that his thoughtless and insolent act caused such inconvenience to a man of honor. We're happy to note his watchful attitude towards his work, but in his excitement to be loyal to his duty, he's taken a step too far. In the future, he needs to be vigilant about that."

The lawyers jumped up in joy at hearing this verdict. Pandit Alopidin walked out of the court with a smile, as his relatives showered money all around him. The sea of generosity swelled with high tide, and their force shook the foundation of Justice and law. When Vanshidhar came out of the courtroom, sarcastic comments poured upon him from all corners. In a mocking gesture, the peons bowed their heads. Each harsh word, every insulting gesture, filled his heart with remorse. That day he learned a strange, deplorable lesson. Law and education, the mighty titles, long beards, and loose gowns- none of them were worthy of respect.

Vanshidhar had offended the power of wealth. He needed to pay the penalty. Within a week, he received a letter of suspension. He paid heavily for performing his duty with zeal and honesty. Broken-hearted, aggrieved, and carrying all the pain in his heart, he left for home. His father, the old man, was as it is fuming even before his son's predicament. 'I explained everything to him before he left home, but he paid no heed to my words. He's a stubborn boy. We've tolerated the reminders of payment from the wine seller and the butcher. I'm living a saintly life in my old age, with nothing but only a meager salary! I too worked in my time, without hankering after a post, but I worked hard. And here, this fellow wants to show off his honesty! His house may stand in darkness. He'd rather lit a lamp in the mosque. I pity his reasoning! All education has been useless.'

And a few days later, after Vanshidhar reached his home in such a dire state, his old father was beyond himself. "I feel like breaking your head and mine too," he said. For a long time, he wrung his hands in helplessness. In anger, he uttered some harsh words. If Vanshidhar stayed there, anger would have erupted. His old mother also felt sad, as her desire to visit the holy places of Jagannath and Rameswaram turned to dust. And his wife did not talk to him for days.

A week passed in this manner. One evening, when the old Munshi was sitting, counting his beads, a well-decked chariot came and stopped near his door. Decorated with green and pink screens, it was drawn by a pair of bullocks who sported blue threads around their neck, and whose horns were topped with bronze. Several servants accompanied the cart, carrying *lathis* (long, heavy bamboo sticks, used as baton) on their shoulders.

The old Munshi walked briskly to welcome the visitor, who was none other than pandit Alopidin. Bowing in front of him, he cajoled him with charming words. "It is our great fortune that you've arrived at our door. You're like a god to us, but we can't show our face to you. It is blackened by our son. He's an unlucky one, or else why would I be ashamed to face you? May God keep a couple childless than giving them a son like this!"

Alopidin said, "No Sir, don't speak like that."

Astonished, the old Munshi said, "How else should I refer to a son like him?"

In a fond voice, Alopidin said, "There aren't many examples of people who enhance the glory of their lineage by standing unflinchingly by their ideals to preserve their righteousness."

Turning to Vanshidhar, pandit Alopidin said, "Don't treat my words as flattery. I need not take so much trouble to laud you. I didn't come so far, only to flatter you. That night, you had the power to arrest me. Today I've come here on my free will to court arrest. I've come across thousands of affluent people in my life; I have dealings with thousands of influential officials. I have enslaved each of them with the power of money. Only you defeated me. Allow me to say something to you today."

Vanshidhar saw Alopidin approaching him, and he welcomed him courteously. But he didn't forget his self-respect. Presuming that Alopidin came there to further humiliate and insult him, he didn't apologize. On the contrary, he felt frustrated observing his father's servile attitude. But Alopidin's words washed away the malice in his heart.

He cast a fleeting glance towards Alopidin and noticed the goodwill he carried with himself. His pride made way for contrition. In a shy voice, he said, "You speak generously about me. Please forgive me for the disrespectful behavior I showed towards you. The shackles of righteousness were binding me. Otherwise, I'm your humble servant and would willingly obey your orders."

Humbly, Alopidin said, "You refused to hear my prayers on the riverbank. But today you'll have to listen to me."

Vanshidhar replied, "I'm not worthy of serving you. Yet, if there's a situation where I may, I'll surely do my best."

Alopidin brought out a judicial paper duly stamped and placed it before Vanshidhar. "Please accept this position and put your signature on this paper. I'm a brahmin, I shall not budge from your door until you fulfil my wish."

As Vanshidhar read the paper, his eyes brimmed with tears of gratitude. Pandit Alopidin had appointed him the manager of all his estate. He'd receive a pay of Rs. Six thousand per annum and a daily allowance on top of it. He would have a horse to ride, a bungalow to live in, and servants free of cost.

In tremulous tones, Vanshidhar replied, "Panditji, I lack words to praise your generosity. But to be honest, I'm not worthy of having such a prime position."

Laughing, Alopidin said, "At the moment, I'm actually searching for an 'unworthy' fellow, just like you!"

In a grave voice, Vanshidhar replied, "I'm your humble servant, anyhow. It'll be my good luck to serve someone as honorable and nice person as you. But I'm neither learned, nor wise, nor do I possess qualities that can make up for the deficiencies I have. This post requires someone who's far-sighted and very experienced."

Alopidin took out the pen from the pen holder and, handing it to Vanshidhar, he said, "I don't need learning, nor experience, nor sagacity, not even expertise. I've already noted the virtues of these qualities. Now, I've found such a rare pearl that reduces the brightness of capability and wisdom. Please take this pen, put your signature, without thinking much. I pray to God that He may forever keep you the same unflinching, harsh, but dutiful Inspector, committed to righteousness!"

Vanshidhar's eyes pooled with tears. In his small heart, he could hardly contain such immense gratitude. His eyes full of reverence towards Panditji, he signed the contract with trembling hands.

Delighted, Alopidin embraced him.

Munshi Premchand

A Winter's Night
Puus ki raat

Halku came in, and said to his wife, "Sahna has come. Get me the money that I gave to you. I will give it to him. At least we will then live in peace."

Munni, his wife, was sweeping the floor. She turned back and said, "We've only three rupees. If you give it to him, how will we buy the blanket? How will we survive the brutal wintry nights while guarding the crops? Tell him we will pay during the next harvest."

For a moment, Halku stood undecided. The month of *puus* (The corresponding December-January month in the Gregorian calendar) was almost at the door. Without a blanket, it would be impossible for him to guard his crops in the field at night. But he also knew that the moneylender Sahna would not relent without the money. He would threaten, abuse and even beat him up. It was better to die in the frosty night outside than facing the abuses hurled by the moneylender. He wanted to be rid of the noose.

With this thought in mind, he dragged his hefty body (which was in contrast to his name 'halku', that meant light-weight!) near to his wife. Flattering her a bit, he said, "Bring the money. Let us get rid of this trouble. I'll devise some other means to get the blanket."

Munni squirmed away from him. Arching her eyes, she said, "I know all about your other means. Let me also know what other means will you employ? Will someone donate a blanket free of cost to you? God knows how much we owe him that the debt never goes down. I say, why don't you stop farming the land? You are killing yourself by toiling hard in the fields. But when harvest comes, we've to give it away to him. Seems like we are born only to pay our debts! I will not give the money to you. No, I won't."

His voice ringing with gloom, Halku asked, "What should I do? Face his abuses?"

"Why should he abuse you? Is he the king?" asked Munni, shouting. She was furious.

But the moment she uttered the words, her taut eyebrows slackened. The truth in Halku's words stared back at her face, like the ferocious eyes of an animal.

She walked up to the alcove in the wall and brought the money to Halku. Placing the three rupees on Halku's palm, she said to him, "You should stop tilling the fields from now on. We shall feed ourselves working as labourers. At least, that way, we would not face such insults. What kind of work is this? Bring home some money after toiling hard and that too we must give away to these people. Not to mention these ugly insults."

Halku took the money. He walked outside, feeling as if he was giving away a part of his heart. Bit by bit, he had saved up those three rupees from his wages to buy a blanket. He had to give them away now. With each step that he was taking, the helplessness of his situation was pressing hard upon his mind.

2

It was the dark, wintry night of *puus*! Even the stars in the dark sky seemed to shiver and freeze in the cold. Halku was on the edge of his field, under the shelter provided by the sugar-cane leaves on his bamboo cot. Wrapped in his old, thick bedcover, he sat shivering in cold. Under his cot, his companion, the dog Jabra, put his mouth into his coiling body, and whimpered in cold. None of them could sleep on that chilly night.

Folding his knees up to his neck, Halku asked Jabra, "Jabra, are you feeling cold? I told you to stay at home, warm on the pile of haystack. Why did you come here? Now face this biting chill. What can I do? Did you think I came here to have a sumptuous meal? Is that why you came running behind me? Now in the name of your grandmother, suffer this."

Jabra wagged his tail, and he let out a long whimper. Then, stretching his body, he fell silent. His dog-sense perhaps understood his master could not sleep hearing his moans and whimpers.

Stretching out his hand, Halku caressed Jabra's back. "Don't come with me from tomorrow, you'll die of cold. God knows from where this westerly wind is bringing this frosty iciness. Let me get up and make another *chillum* (a short pipe usually made of clay to smoke tobacco) for myself. I've to pass this night somehow. I've already consumed eight *chillum*. Well, the pleasure of being a farmer, you can say! And then there are those fortunate few! If the cold went anywhere near them, the surrounding heat would drive it away. What not they have? Thick blankets, bedsheets, and quilts! The cold does not dare come near them. How strange our life is! We toil hard, while others enjoy."

Halku got up and, taking a cinder from the pit nearby, he lit the *chillum*. Jabra, too, sat up.

Taking a swig from his pipe, Halku asked, "Would you like to try it, Jabra? It won't lessen the cold, but it'll bring pleasure to the mind, at least."

Jabra stared at him, his eyes brimming over with tenderness.

Halku said, "Manage the cold today. From tomorrow I will bring a pile of hay stack and spread it here. Sit inside that, then you won't feel so cold."

Jabra kept his paws on Halku's knees and brought his face closer to his master. His warm breath caressed Halku's face.

After smoking his *chillum,* Halku lay on his cot again, and this time he made his mind to sleep. However, the moment he tried to court sleep, shivering came over him. He turned on his sides from this side to the other, but the icy cold seemed to clamp his heart like an evil spirit.

When nothing worked, he lifted Jabra up and, caressing his head, he made the dog sleep on his lap. The dog reeked of foul smell, but holding his body close on his lap, Halku felt at peace, a feeling he had not experienced for months. Jabra perhaps felt there as comfortable as in heaven, and in Halku's innocent heart there was not a trace of revulsion for the dog. He would take his close relative or friend in an embrace with similar affection. The sorry state in which he found himself did not hurt him any longer now. No, this unique friendship which he shared with Jabra had almost opened up every door of his heart and spirit, and each pore of his being shone in brilliant radiance.

Suddenly Jabra heard some animal's footstep. This close alliance with Halku had filled him up with a special alertness, which ignored the icy fangs of the bitter wind. Jumping up, he ran out of the shed and started barking with full urgency. Several times, Halku tried in a friendly manner to coax him back into the shed, but he did not come. He ran around the field and continued to bark. For a moment, even if he came to Halku, he would at once turn back and run. Duty seemed to brim over in his heart, almost like longings.

3

An hour passed by. Night flared up the cold with the icy winds. Halku got up, brought his knees closer to his chest and dig his head within, yet the frosty cold did not diminish a bit. It seemed blood had frozen in his body, and through his veins ice coursed, instead of blood. He looked up at the sky to understand how long the night would last. The constellation of *Saptrishi* (Ursa Major) was only half-way up in the night sky. Dawn would arrive once the constellation moved up. Over one fourth of the night remained.

At a stone's throw distance from Halku's fields, there was a mango orchard. It was autumn, and the dry leaves fell off, making a pile under the trees. Halku thought of collecting the leaves, lit them up, and get some warmth from the fire. If anyone saw me collecting the leaves on this dark night, he would mistake me to be a ghost! But he wondered if some animal sat hiding inside those leaves. And yet, it was now so cold that he could not withstand it any more.

He went to the lentil field nearby, pulled up a few stalks, and made a broom by tying them together. Then, carrying a burning cow dung cake in his hand, he walked towards the mango orchard. When Jabra saw him coming, he came near, wagging his tail.

"It is now impossible to bear the cold, Jabru," said Halku. "Come, let us go to the orchard, find some dry leaves and warm ourselves up. When we feel cosy and warm, we will come back here and get some sleep. It is going to be a long night."

Jabra gave his assent with a whimper and ran ahead toward the orchard.

It was pitch dark in the orchard. The merciless wind thrashed the dry leaves and marched ahead. Dew drops dripped from the trees.

All of a sudden, a whiff of henna flowers wafted through the night, carried over by the breeze.

"What a beautiful fragrance is that, Jabru," said Halku. "I'm sure you smell that too."

Jabra got hold of a bone on the ground. He chewed on it.

Keeping down the fire, Halku began collecting the leaves. Within a few minutes, he gathered an enormous pile of them. His hands were almost numb. His bare feet had no feeling left in them. And he kept busy in stocking up the pile. He wished to burn the cold to ashes with this pile.

Soon, the pile of leaves flared up in a blaze. The flames of fire rose high up, almost touching the tips of the tree branches. The trees in that orchard appeared to stand, carrying the deep darkness on their heads against the flickering light of flame. In the endless sea of darkness, the flame looked like a boat trembling and rocking.

Halku sat in front of the bonfire, taking its warmth. In a moment, he took out his garment, kept it under his arms, and spread his legs before the fire, as if provoking the fire to do what it can. His victory over the mighty power of cold brought a sense of triumph into his heart; he could not suppress it for long.

He asked Jabra, "Why, Jabra, now you're not feeling cold, right?"

Jabra whined in reply. As if he was saying, "Are we going to be cold forever?"

"If we had thought of this solution, we would not have suffered in cold."

Jabra wagged his tail.

"Come, let us jump through this fire and see who can cross it over. And son, if you get burned, I won't be able to treat you!" Jabra stared at that bonfire with frightened eyes. "And don't tell Munni about this tomorrow. Otherwise she will fight with me!"

Saying this, he jumped over the bonfire and crossed it over to the other side. His legs grazed over the fire, but it did not harm him. Jabra only circled around the fire and came and stood near him.

Halku said, "No, this isn't fair. Jump above the flames." And then he jumped over again and landed on the other side of the burning fire.

4

The leaves were burnt, and darkness returned to the orchard. The fire still burned slowly under the ashes. Stoked by the bursts of wind, it awakened for a while, but soon closed its eyes.

Halku wrapped himself well with the sheet and, sitting beside the warm ashes, he hummed a song. His body had now warmed up, but as the surrounding cold increased, a state of lethargy caught him in its grip.

Jabra barked aloud and ran towards the field. Halku felt that a herd of animal had entered his field. Perhaps those were the bunch of *neelgais (Asian antelope),* and he could clearly hear their footsteps, trampling and running in his field. Soon he could also hear them chewing his crop.

In his heart, he said, "No, Jabra is there. In his presence, no animal can get into my fields. He is going to claw them down. I'm just imagining things! I'm not hearing anything anymore."

He shouted aloud. "Jabra, Jabra!"

Jabra kept on barking, but he did not come to him.

Then again, he heard the animals munching and grazing in his field. This time, the sounds did not dupe him. But he felt it impossible to leave his place. He was sitting all snugged up in warmth. To move from his place in this frosty night and run after those animals seemed quite reckless to him. He sat in his place and did not move from there.

Jabra barked again. The animals were grazing the field. The harvest was ready. What a good harvest it was! But the evil animals ruined them completely!

Determined to chase them away, Halku took a few steps. But just then, a cold burst of wind bit through him like a scorpion. He came back, sat beside the fire, and stoked the dying embers to warm himself again.

Jabra barked himself hoarse while the *neelgais* grazed the entire harvest.   Surrendering to fate, Halku sat in silence near the fire. The strings of lethargy bound him up tightly on all sides.

He covered himself with the sheet and went to sleep near the fire on that warm soil.

Early morning, when his eyes opened, sun was shining brightly around him. Munni was saying, "Will you keep on sleeping like this? You slept here in peace and there the harvest got ruined."

Getting up, Halku asked, "Are you coming from the field?"

"Yes," said Munni. "The animals ravaged the crops

completely. Who sleeps like this? What was the use of you camping in the field?"

Halku came up with an excuse. "I was almost dying here. And all you are worried about are the crops. Only I know how severe a pain I had in my stomach!"

Both then walked towards their field. They saw the entire field was ravaged and destroyed. Only Jabra lay lifeless under the shed.

Both of them stared ahead at their fields. Munni was heartbroken, but Halku appeared happy.

Concerned, Munni said, "Now we have to work as laborers and pay off our debts."

"At least I won't have to sleep here, out in the cold," replied Halku with a cheerful face.

Rajsekhar Basu

Young Hearts' Club
Kochi Sansad

Reports coming from the Alipore weather office were rather encouraging. It said that the low pressure building over the *Sagar Islands* (An island in the delta of Ganges in southeast Bengal in India) had melted away. It meant there was no possibility of rains anymore. The shadows of cloud could not hide the sun from peeping through the blue canopy. The sun shone brighter, wearing the color of bronze. It made my wife quite fearless, and she had put out our quilts and blankets to be warmed under the sun. The mellowed chill in the late-night air made it obligatory to snuggle closer under the blankets. In the vegetable market, skinny but fresh cauliflowers were being sold, four at the price of one rupee. The price of potatoes was higher than those of *potol*, the pointed gourds. Early autumn's arrival imprinted itself not only throughout the natural landscape but also in the recesses of our mind and soul. This was indeed the time when, in the past, the kings went out to vanquish other lands.

As the courts were closed, I'd no clients either. From

the nearby railway tracks, I heard the whistle of a passing train. Astonished, I saw my older son flinging aside his geometry book; he was, with full concentration, studying the railway timetable. My younger one seemed fascinated by engines. Like an engine, he chugged, swaying and waving his arms, and gave out a loud call, *"Chug-chug! Coooo! Chug-Chug!"* It agitated me.

Where should I go for a vacation this year? I wondered. A few good-natured friends advised me to visit the ancestral village and spend time in uplifting the village life. I admit with a shameful heart that such an idealistic goal wouldn't harmonize with me. Of course, I was aware of my duties; but I lacked the wish to fulfil it. In my mind, only one thought reigned supreme: where could I go on a holiday?

There were indeed many modes of transport; one could go on foot, or by bullock cart, a motor car, boat or even by a ship. But I preferred a journey by train. I believed the train to be the king of transport, and the best among them was for sure the E.I.R (Eastern Indian railway). My friends are, of course, not as passionate as me. They say, "Your passion and preference for something made by the British is rather crude."

My answer to them is: "Well, yes, the British started the railways, but they aren't paying for it. Today we're eulogizing them, but there used to be a time when they watched our deeds in awe. Just wait another two hundred years, our time will come. We'll have trains running from one planet to other, and they would stare at us in amazement. And then, even if they paid us the fare, we'd not take them along."

Bengal's beautiful land, with its rivers, both big and small, is soothing to us. And its vagrant bushes, the sweet smell of the dried cow-dung cakes, the balmy incense of *jui* (jasmine) flowers, rising from the ponds covered with water-hyacinth, are no less comforting to us. But in these shimmering days of early autumn, my heart yearns to make long distance travels, tearing through the plains, speeding to my destination. The Punjab Mail, rattling and cutting sweeps forward, and the sprawling fields, the cluster of palm trees, small hillocks, ever changing landscape, jumping from scene to scene. Brief halts at stations. *Paan-beedi*-cigarette, (Betel leaf mixture and thin cigarette filled with tobacco) warm tea, *Puri-Kachuri*, (deep-fried bread and snacks) *roti-kebab* (Indian flat bread and meat). And the next moment, we're galloping away again! Telegraph poles rush by us, so does the sugarcane fields, and the small, tiny rivers would coil and disappear in the blink of an eye, through the haze, while in the distance our eyes would carve out the green forest, looming in view. And through the open window, the sudden smell of *Chhatim* flowers-strong and sweet- would waft through, mingling with the smell of the coal from the coal engine. And all the while, the golden orb in the western sky would try to keep pace, running and racing with our train.

On the opposite bench, the pot-bellied merchant is already snoring. The English passenger on the bunk above my head is drinking something from his bottle. I'm sitting on two layers of blankets, my stomach already full of yummy treats, while more such savories are waiting in the wicker basket. Such a rattling and a clattering of the metallic parts of the train, as it tears forward with its rhythmic chugging, while I lay flat on my back, swaying wildly with the clang and clank, as if performing a *tandava* (A divine dance performed by the Hindu God Shiva)! Ah, it is as if I'm in a paradise!

This senseless attraction for the railway. What prompted it, I wonder? What was that secret wish that hid in the chambers of my inner mind, like a coiling snake, triggering such monstrous plans? I dared not ask about this to my psychologist brother, Girin Bose. Rather promptly, I decided- I would go to Dalhousie (A hill station in the Northern Indian state of Himachal Pradesh). Alone, on an invitation offered by a Punjabi friend. I thought I shall bribe my wife by allowing her to go to as many theaters as she wished to. But then.... man proposes, woman disposes!

While I was dusting the large suitcase, my wife barged into the room, as swift as a streak of lightning. "What, what, what?" she queried.

I must explain a particular point here in secret. My wife's knowledge of English grammar extended to the First book. But thanks to my impertinent brother in-laws, from them she picked up a few commonplace words and used them generously wherever possible.

Stammering, I began, "Well, I was thinking of spending a few days in the mountains, you know, kind of holiday...... I'm feeling kind of bit low, you see."

"Kind of low? What do you mean kind of low? Oh, I see. You're planning to go alone. Have I now become such a tremendous burden to you? What would you do alone in the mountains, pray? Meditate?"

I noted the dark clouds gather on her face with alarm. I understood a volcano was about to erupt at any moment. In a flash, I changed my track. "God forbid! What're you saying? How can I meditate without you?"

My words were like a mantra, and those cleared away the nuisance of the impending smoke at once. Smiling, my wife asked, "To which mountain?"

"To Dalhousie. It's quite far away."

"Hang Dalhousie. Let's go to Darjeeling (A small hill station, once a famous British summer resort, located in the foothills of the Himalayas in the Indian state of West Bengal). I've to buy another thirty stone necklaces, and four dozen brooms. And that boa necklace I bought last time, the one that resembles the caterpillar, I never got the chance to wear it at all. And yes, that wheel shaped diamond brooch. Who's there to see me wearing those on your stupid Dalhousie mountain? No one. In Darjeeling, we'd meet so many friends. Tuni-didi and her sister-in-law are there; and Sarojini, Suku -Mashi have also reached there. And I assume Monki Mitra's wife, with their brood of thirteen children, has gone there, too."

It was almost impossible to refute the logic in her arguments. And so, our destination changed to Darjeeling.

XXXXX

Rain and clouds were embracing Darjeeling when we reached there. I lost the desire to go out, but staying indoors was even worse. One day, after having my breakfast, I set off for a walk, wearing my heavy boots and covering myself from head to toe in a mackintosh. Calcutta road was empty of people, and as I strolled through the avenue, I thought how terrible it was to be alone in this land of clouds, when....

My fate, until then, was resembling the protagonist in Tagore's story, who also wandered idly on this same road in Darjeeling. Here, on this street, he then came across the daughter of Golam Kader Khan, the nawab of Badraun. But alas! my fate differed from his. Instead of the Nawab's daughter, I came across uncle Nokur. An attorney in Dumraon by profession, everyone called him 'mama'- the uncle!

By the side of a gorge, on a bench, I found him sitting. He held an umbrella over his head, a woolen scarf was wrapped around his neck, he wore an overcoat, sported a frowning look, and his face showed extreme displeasure. The moment he saw me, he said, "Is that you, Brajen?"

"Yes, Sir. Is everyone well at home? What brings you to Darjeeling? What is Keshto doing these days? Is he still in Benares?" I asked after Keshto, who was Nokur mama's nephew. He had lost parents early in his life. His father was a well reputed doctor. In his mid-twenties, Keshto was rather eccentric in his behavior, and did not treat his uncle with much respect. However, he reserved some regard for me.

"I'll explain everything," Nokur mama replied. "But first, you answer this question- why do they all come to Darjeeling? If they want to have a cold, why, they can buy several kilos of ice in Calcutta, shall cost only a rupee! Spreading an oilcloth on the slabs of ice can also do the trick, right! It'll be cheaper too! But no, people prefer to visit higher altitudes. Or else, one can't satisfy these modern, luxury-prone youngsters. Well, they can climb those tall palm trees, if they're looking for high altitudes! The unworthy stupid ones..." he vented out.

Once, in the ancient times, when the earth was but born, *Vishwakarma* (the artisan deity in the Hindu scriptures) had squeezed it so well, that the earth still kept the marks of his fingers as mountains, valleys, rivers and oceans. It was the result of his great pinch that the tall Himalayas rose on our earth. But little indulgence by God made the man arrogant, as he climbed the peak of the mountain and built the city Darjeeling there. Nokur mama disapproved that. A believer in God, man's verbosity, quite displeased him.

"There's some joy even in distress, you know Nokur mama," I replied. "And so, people these days spend money and buy happiness. It's the same in this case too.

Since Darjeeling exists, people are thinking of climbing mountains and are not hesitating to spend some money visiting the city. Thankfully, we also have landslides."

Panicked, uncle jumped from his place by the side of the gorge, and with haste took a safer position on the street. "Let them rot in hell!" he commented. "Is this even a place for a gentleman? Now and then, there's rain, and each time you venture out of home, you've to climb the slope. After two steps, one must stop to catch one's breath. There're no stairs either. In case you slip, you're sure to break your bones. You pant as you walk; and your teeth chatter as you stop. *Why* on earth must one visit such a place?"

Nokur mama looked around himself with an irate glance. Had it been those mythological days and mama had been one of those revered holy men, with the ability to burn anything only with a mere look, by now the entire city of Darjeeling would be in ashes, burning like Sahara, the desert. I asked, "Then why are you here?"

"Not out of my wish," replied he. "You know how Keshto is like. His education is over. He should now marry, look after his property. Thank God, he doesn't need to work for a living! But no, he wouldn't do that. For a few days, he spent his time on drawing and painting. Then, he started an *aamshotto* (sun dried mango pulp mixed with sugar) factory and wasted some money. After that, he went to Calcutta, created a group of young people, like himself, and formed a group, kind of a club, like an assembly. Then, he went to Bombay, and from there he sent me an urgent telegram. An order, it was. *Go to the Moonshine villa in Darjeeling at once. Stay there*, it said. You see, he's coming here to get married. What could I do? My nephew is rich, and I had to oblige. When I reached Moonshine Villa, pandemonium had broken out there. The bridegroom's party was already present there. The entire club called- *Kochi Sansad*- is in Darjeeling. And Keshto is their president!"

"Has he found a bride?"

"No, No. Who knows, perhaps he'd marry a local Lepcha woman, or maybe a Bhutani girl!"

"And the members of his club? Don't they know anything?"

"Nothing at all. And even if they knew and tried to inform me about it, I'd not understand a word. To me, their conversation is very puzzling. The only good thing about them is, they are foodies. They like good food. I have meals with them, nothing more. Well, Keshto is arriving this evening. If you drop in then, you'd be able to meet those clowns yourself and see what's going on."

Of course, I was aware of *Kochi Sansad*- a club for the young hearts. Their secretary, Pelob Roy, was from our neighborhood. His original name was Pelaram, but there came a change in him. He grew his hair long, turned rather dainty, shaved his moustache off, and wore his hair in a puffed fashion on both sides, much like those sported by the lady typists. Then, wearing a silken *kurta* and a silken shawl, matching it with green, ethnic *Nagra* shoes (a type of footwear common in Bengal), and displaying a red fountain pen in his breast pocket, he left for Madhupur.

There, meeting his vice-chancellor Sir Ashutosh Mukherjee, he requested him to change his name in the university register from Pelaram to Pelob Roy. Grabbing a volume of a thick encyclopedia, Sir Ashutosh chased him away. After that, Pelaram fled from there, locked away his BA degree, and from then he turned into Pelob Roy, discarding his degree forever. As far as I knew, it was he who established the *Kochi Sansad- Young hearts' club*, although Keshto bore the expenses. I do not know with what vision in mind they formed this club. But rumour had it they were rather picky about their members. And the process of initiation was also quite an elaborate, and terrible one. Holding hands with all the existing members, the new member had to take sixteen difficult oaths while consuming sixteen tins of cigarettes, not to mention umpteen cups of tea!

By then, it was late, and the clouds too had scattered away. I promised uncle Nokur to be there at the *Moonshine-villa* in the evening and took his leave.

XXXXX

Coiling three emerald and ruby necklaces, each worth one rupee and twenty-five paisa, on her slender neck, my wife asked me, "So, how do I look?"

"Oh, fabulous. Just as the wife of another man."

"You're a cad," exclaimed my wife. "Are there only other men's wives in your fancy?"

"*Arre*, why're you getting mad?" I tried to explain. "Extra-marital love is not an ordinary thing; it is a class apart. Not every Tom, Dick and Harry would understand its worth. But if a man perceives his wife in the same light- you know, discovering new things each day in her, and experiencing each time that 'yet not attained' feeling, then he has progressed much in his seeking. Look at *Radha and Krishna* (Radha and Krishna are collectively known as the combined forms of feminine and masculine realities of God in Hinduism.), they are the ideal lovers. Freud said..."

"Damn Freud- and forget Radha and Krishna. For someone as ordinary as me, *Ram and Sita* (Ram is a major deity in Hinduism and Sita is his wife) are good enough."

"But Ram wanted to burn Sita, not once, but twice. What about that?"

"Oh, that's because his subjects demanded that. Those people, in that age, were all rascals."

"Then why didn't he just handover the throne to Bharat, and leave for the forest again, together with Sita?"

"He could have, but those same foolish subjects wouldn't wish to let him go. That's the reason."

"Well, you're a better lawyer than me! I thank you on behalf of Sri Ram. It was his great luck he had a wife like Sita. If he had been married to you, the entire populace of Ayodhya would be hanged by now!"

My wife at once asked, "Why? Am I a *rakhashi* (a she-demon), like Shurpanakha or Taraka?"

"Sita was a docile and demure lady. Not as demanding as you."

"Oh really? What about her demand for the golden deer, then? Have you any idea how much it would have weighed? In its hollow state, too, the deer would have weighed at least five kilos."

"Ok, all right, you win. But have you heard the news? Keshto is coming here. Our Keshto from Banaras. He's coming here to get married."

"Hurrah! Thank goodness, at least I brought some jewelries! But how'd he get married in the month of *Ashwin* (the seventh month of the Hindu calendar)? There're no auspicious days in this month."

"Does that matter if your love is strong? Every day and each moment is a favorable moment. But no one yet knows who his bride is. Perhaps he's still searching for one, although his friends have all arrived."

"Gad!" my wife exclaimed. "I had once heard that his father wished him to get married to Tuni-didi's sister-in-law. She's grown up to be a pretty lady, and she's now here in Darjeeling. Her parents are dead, now her brother Bhuban is her guardian. Bhuban is our Tuni-didi's husband."

"I do not know if Keshto has thought about her. Who knows what goes through his mind? Not even Lord Shiva can predict that! Anyway, I'll go to Keshto's place in the evening to find out everything."

XXXXXX

On a dreamy evening, we walked through a quiet, deserted road. The city bathed in lights, all around me, even above me, and beneath me. In layer after layer, lights shimmered and glowed. On the wayside, in the bushes and shrubs, the crickets chorused together tremulously, their buzzing triggering a final crescendo. The moon had climbed on a clear night, there was no trace of mist.

And there stood the Moonshine villa.

What was that noise? There were no foxes in Darjeeling. Perhaps the Maharaja of Burdwan brought a few foxes along with him to Darjeeling. But all those foxes were now at the Moonshine villa? Oh, no. Those were not the foxes. Those were the members of *the young hearts' club*- singing out loud. The words were unintelligible to me. I half guessed them. The young hearts seemed to pour out their heart's pain in a song for some unknown, unheard of young lady. Oh God, Nokur uncle, is this what luck had in store for you?

Watching me come in, the group stopped singing. I could not see either Uncle or Keshto anywhere nearby. I heard Keshto had reached Darjeeling, but nobody knew where had put up. They expected him to appear soon at Moonshine Villa.

With a warm greeting, Pelob Roy offered me a seat and introduced me to the other members. Those were:

Shiharan Sen
Bigolito Banerjee
Okinchit Kar
Hootash Halder
Dodul Dey
Lalima Pal (M)

I wondered if their parents had given these names or the members themselves chose these names? I thought of asking, but found it hard to cross the barrier of courtesy. Lalima Pal wasn't a woman, and to prevent the confusion, he had added "M" for male against his name!

Suddenly, the door opened, and Uncle Nokur came in. And who was that following him? Could it be Keshto? I realized then that I wasn't the only astonished one in the room; the entire group stared at him. Hootash, their youngest member, who had just started to smoke, seemed daunted by Keshto's entry.

For Keshto's appearance, from head to toe, seemed unusual, a declaration of dissent against all the accepted forms and norms of dressing, as adorned by the common Bengali gentlemen. His head was almost shorn of hair. He had no moustache, but he sported a goatee. On his body, he wore a short green shirt with white, large polka dots. He wore a belt on his waist, and a purple *dhoti* (a type of sarong, tied in a manner that outwardly resembles loose trousers). On his feet, he wore long socks with boots. He carried a knapsack on his back, tied with a strap and carried a wooden stick in his hand.

I was the first one to break the silence. "Hello Keshto, what is this horror now?"

"That's what it will feel in the beginning," he replied. "But after hearing out my explanation, you'd understand what I've done is right. Brajen-da, life is no child's play, it is both art and efficiency."

"Ok, but why do you have such an appearance?"

"Listen! Man doesn't need so much hair; I've kept only as much as I need to save myself from extreme heat and cold. And now the beard. This kind of beard, as you see on my face, they call it 'imperial', and its job is to balance the nose. People wear dark shirts over white *dhotis*. That looks awful, it just makes one look top-heavy. Look at my clothes- plum violet and sage green, with white spots. This brings both color contrast and harmony. I've now ordered for a few shorts, with printed design at the hip. It would improve the waistline immensely. And this stick, look at this! With this, one can kill a tiger. And in this knapsack, I carry everything that I might need. I'm independent, I'm self-reliant and I'm without a concern!"

Pausing here, Keshto took out two cigarettes from two different packets, and started smoking both. "Can you do this? One is Virginia and the other one is Turkish. And both are blending within me."

I saw Nokur's uncle flopping down without a word. His eyes were closed, and I could very well visualize the flames of anger burning slowly but surely in his heart.

Pelob Roy spoke up. "Keshto, you're the President of our young heart group. What made you do this?"

"I was young and tender all right, but now the time has ripened."

"Of course," I added. "Or else you'd be parched dry. Anyway, Keshto, I heard you're going to get married?"

"Oh yes, that's what brings me here. I'm glad that you too are here. But before anything, I'd like to talk a bit about love."

"Uncle Nokur, better go upstairs and retire straight to bed," I suggested to Uncle. "No need to expose yourself further to a chilly night. I'll inform you whatever transpires here...... Well then, Keshto, what is love? I say, why not have a cup of tea along with the discussion?"

"Boda! Boda!" Pelob Roy called out.

Boda was Keshto's servant, born in the Kshatriya (warrior class) clan, a clear descendant of the moon. His face was as round as the moon itself. Pelob ordered him to bring ten cups of tea.

Keshto spoke about love. "Many great people have expressed their opinions about love. In *Chandidas's* (a medieval poet of Bengal) words, love is bitter sweet. The Russian poet, Vodkawoski says that love is a drug, albeit a mediocre drug. Metsnikoff says, love increases your life span by a few years, but for better results you must try buttermilk. Madam De Siyan says, Love is the only weapon using which a woman may take away everything from a man. Omar Khyam writes, love is like a drink made of moonlight, but one must add a bit of liquor to it. And Henry the Eighth says, Love is immortal. If you kill one woman in love, ten more will come up. Freud says love is like a civilized plaster over man's animalistic passions. Havelock Ellis says..."

"Enough!" I cried. "What's your opinion, let's hear that."

"In my opinion, love is nothing but a deception, through which men and women deceive each other."

A collective moan rose from the young hearts' assembly. Placing a hand on his heart, Hootash said, "It's painful!"

"Why are you making such noises, Huto?" Keshto asked. "Have you smoked too many cigarettes? Don't smoke so much!"

We all heard a purling sound, and it came from Lalima Pal's throat. The sound seemed similar to the one that those Japanese clocks made before they struck the hour. Perhaps his voice was a bit mucus infested. To cure this, he used to take a special medicine of herbs mashed with Cuckoo's eggs; however, since he did not find such exotic ingredients, his treatment had run into a pause in Darjeeling. Keshto encouraged him to speak his opinion on love.

"I guess Love is a.... kind of... kind of..." he began with a stammer.

".... an earthquake?" I suggested.

"Indeed, yes. Exactly." Keshto butted in. "Love is an earthquake, a cloudburst, kind of Niagara Falls, that is high, mighty and also perilous, it is a sudden danger- that mars your common sense."

Lalima, with his whizzing, possibly wished to differ with him, but fell quiet as he realized it would be useless.

"Then why do you wish to get married? Are you going to get a lot of money in a dowry?" I asked.

"Not a cent. My idea in getting married is more to set an example. An example of an ideal marriage. In our society, we mainly see two types of marriages- one is where marriage comes before love. This is the backdated Hindu marriage. And the other one is where love precedes marriage. There's a courtship involved. In my eyes, both are wrong. After marriage, if the couple aren't able to like each other, how can there be love? The second one, where people are in love first, and then they marry- is also unsuitable, because during courtship both hide their flaws. And after marriage, when the faults come into light, then it is usually too late."

"What's new in this? These are well-known facts. What's your idea, tell us that."

Keshto replied, "In my system the element of love will

be chucked out of courtship, because the very presence of love forces the two sides to hide their genuine characters. There would be a period of courtship, sans love. I'd need a man and a woman, both educated, detached, with a prudent mind; and a sensible, experienced mediator who'd judge the views, opinions of both the sides. I've made a list of ninety-three topics. It includes dressing sense, eating habits, sleeping patterns, reading preferences, liking for art and culture, friend selection habits, amusement and entertainment activities, etc. Most of the time, a couple fights over these topics. If at first, we sort all these points out and one can reach a consensus, then there can't be any problems later. But remember, love can't enter this process, then things will be messy. Let there be love only towards the end of the process. I don't mind that! Till now people were used to courtship, my process is 'high-courtship.'!"

"Sounds more like court-martial," I remarked. "All right, we have heard your system. But have you found the girl? Which girl would go along with your experiment? Besides, I'd say, don't even worry about love. One look at your appearance, and love would gallop away as fast and as far away as possible."

"I've been able to select and finalize my would-be bride today," Keshto replied.

"Who is that unfortunate lady?"

"Padmamadhu Bose, Bhuvan Bose's sister."

"Oh, really? She's our Tuni-didi's sister-in-law. Seems like my wife guessed it right! But I heard that your marriage with Padma was discussed earlier, too. Would this matter not prejudice your case?"

"Not at all," Keshto explained. "Both of us are rather objective in this matter. Brajen-da, you must be the arbiter.

You're experienced in both legal and matrimonial laws; you'd be able to question correctly."

"I am okay with it. I just hope the girl doesn't get angry at me."

"Have no fear, Padma is an intelligent fellow."

"*Intelligent fellow?* But how is she as a woman?"

Keshto answered, "Quite strong, I presume. Padma can walk up to seven miles, play tennis for two hours, have a high muscular index, and rather low fatigue coefficient. She can cook, sew. Other than being logical, she has studied economics too, and doesn't sing loudly or argue too much. Come to Bhuvan Bose's house tomorrow evening- Lovelock Road, Maudlin Cottage."

Giving my word, I left. As I was crossing the gate of Moonshine villa, I heard the cacophony. I assumed the pain and sorrow of the members of the young hearts' assembly coming together and collectively bawling out at Keshto. I didn't linger there anymore.

XXXXXXX

After hearing me out, my wife remarked, "Ripping! This promises to be better than those Parsi plays. I'm sure coming along with you. If it means that I've to spend some money to buy the ticket, I'll do so!"

I replied, "But they won't allow you to be there. High courtship is carried out in ultimate secrecy! Only I, Keshto and Padma would be there in the room."

"I'll eavesdrop!"

"No need. I'll report to you everything later. My ears will be as good as your ears."

"No way. I'll still go."

"But it's rather indecent of you to show such extreme

curiosity about other people's matters! Do you know how Freud would have explained it?" I asked.

"Stop! Don't even utter that worthless's name!" said she.

And so, without no other option in hand, both of us set out for Tuni-didi's house.

XXXXXXX

Tuni-didi and Bhuvan Bose were two opposite characters. The husband was the laziest of them all. Forever sporting his dressing gown, all he did was lounge in his easy chair, reading a newspaper, and smoking cigars. His wife, on the contrary, was deft, prompt, full of energy and was skillful in handling all kinds of chores, from cutting a fish to booking a railway reservation. She preferred doing her own jobs and had not much time for chatting with others. As we entered, she exchanged greeting with us and soon disappeared in the kitchen to make elaborate arrangements for our food. Padma appeared and touched our feet, seeking blessings.

Padma was a lovely woman. I wondered what made Keshto call her as "strong"? She was a tender woman, for God's sake! Not a hammer or a mortar-pestle! I realized Keshto must be the most insensible of the lot of young hearts' club. No matter how much he spoke of love! But I failed to understand why this sweet-looking, intelligent young woman agreed to take part in that asshole's weird plan? Was it to enjoy how Keshto made a fool of himself? To understand a female mind was a tough task; I needed to read up more on it.

I started the high courtship process. From the kitchen, I could hear the amused laughter of Tuni-didi and my wife;

and my nose relished the aroma of the cutlets being fried there. Mustering all my courage, sporting a straight, serious face, I stared at the auspicious task.

"Although in this case, we are not sure who is the petitioner, who is the defendant, nor do we know who the accused is. Yet, all these shall not affect the outcome of this case. We have here two principal witnesses- Keshto and Padma..."

"Brajen-da!" Keshto interfered. "Please don't make a joke about such a serious matter. Let us now start..."

"Why hurry? Let me at first administer the oath, then it can begin. Mr. Keshto, do you agree you harbor no feelings of love for this woman? If you have such feelings, then the case shall stand quashed."

"Not at all. I swear to God I've no feelings of love for Padma. Since she was five and I was ten, I have known her. I see her in the same manner now. The only difference being, then I used to smack her, now I don't!"

"Miss Padma, I will not add injury to your intelligence by asking about your feelings for Keshto. His very appearance is an antidote for love. Keshto, now let me have that list of yours. Oh, ninety-three points! Clothing, eating habits, sleeping habits.... looks like the whole thing would take around fifteen days! Let me ask a few significant questions today. If things look hopeful, then from tomorrow I'd start a systematic interrogation, is that ok? Let us start with food habits first, since that is one of the most important points, no matter what Freud says. Keshto, do you prefer eating chilies?"

"No, I can't stand chilies, or hot food at all."

"And you Padma?"

"I must have chilies; I can't finish my food without it."

"Oh, a rather poor start," I commented. "You get

a cross at the beginning. There can't be two kitchens in a home. We'll decide later if we can make a compromise on this point. Maybe boil the chilly, have both of you eat it, to determine your chilly tolerance. All right, next question. How much sugar do you take in your tea?"

"One spoonful," replied Keshto.

"Seven for me," answered Padma.

"Oh, another cross then. Too bad."

"I can manage with three spoons," said Keshto. "Padma, why don't you climb down a bit from seven spoons?"

"Hey, watch out!" I warned. "Don't influence the opposite party. I'll ask all the questions. Ok, Keshto, what type of mattress would you prefer? Hard or soft?"

"I enjoy sleeping on a hard mattress, almost two inches thick. But I can't sleep on a soft bed."

Padma liked her bed soft. "Soft like butter."

"Going terrible. This is the third cross. Ok, Keshto, what's your opinion on Padma's looks?"

"Not bad," was his reply.

I gave out a shout, the one I reserved to scare the witnesses. "Not so vague, that won't do. Look and then answer!"

Padma blushed. Keshto observed her minutely for a while, and then giving a rather foolish grin, he said, "Oh, she's... she's...... rather pretty! I mean, she's not the girl of yesteryears, she has changed a lot. She is absolutely...."

"That's enough!" I said. "No need to utter further nonsense. Now, Padma you look at him and give your opinion."

Frowning, Padma gave a quick glance at Keshto. "He looks like a clown."

"Oh?" Keshto exclaimed. "All right, I can make some

changes. I can grow my hair an inch longer, and I'll do away with my goatee. Ok, see I'll cover the beard with my hands. Now, look one more time Padma."

Padma giggled out at his attempts.

"Pretty hopeless," I told them. "I can deal with justified objections; but how do I deal with mockery?"

A bit enraged, Keshto said, "It's all your fault! You're making such useless remarks and confusing us!"

"Ok, then have it your way. You may question her yourself."

Taking charge, Keshto rolled up his sleeves. "Padma, look at my arm. These are the biceps, and see, here are the triceps. Do you like the tough, muscular body like mine, or would you prefer the plump, portly figure like Brajen-da? After hearing your opinion, I'd rethink about my appearance."

"Why should your appearance influence me in any way? It's your business, right?" Padma answered. "After all, I'm not hiring you as my watchman!"

"All right! Give me your hand. Let us see how much strength...." saying so, he grabbed Padma's hand.

I was aghast. "What are you doing, Keshto?" I spoke up, objecting to this behavior. "You may not attack the witness! Go, now, sit there. If I'm employed as the mediator, then I'll do what is best."

"Ok, please go ahead with your questions," replied Keshto, rather sheepishly.

"No, I don't see any reason to do that. You both are not compatible at all. And I don't believe we can reach a compromise. So, here's my verdict: *Nappo, nothing doing*. I'm adjourning the case now. Take a year's time to revise your opinions and then come back to this court."

Keshto lost his calm. "You've not understood my

system at all. The way you questioned us, was far from being systematic; it was such a joke. It was wrong of me to appoint you as an arbiter."

I was no less angry. "Look, Keshto, don't act over smart with me. I'm an advocate, I've been practicing for twelve long years, and am married for fifteen years. Not only that, I've also studied human psychology for around a month. I know very well about the compatibility between people. Besides, why are you getting so agitated? Were you not supposed to remain uninvolved and detached? Look at Padma, she's quiet, and composed."

Keshto grumbled. At that point, Tuni-didi's youngest daughter Khuki came in. "What brings you here, lady?" I asked in a somber voice.

Khuki's demand was an exemplary one for the entire womankind. "Do come inside and eat. The *luchis* (a deep-fried flatbread, made of wheat in Bengali homes) are getting cold."

While eating, Keshto kept to himself; he didn't relish his food. After dinner, I returned home alone, for my wife stayed back in Tuni-didi's home.

XXXXXXXXX

Around ten o'clock, the next morning, my wife returned. She went straight to bed, pulling a blanket over her body, wrapping herself tightly in it. With rising horror, I watched her shake within the blanket; soon, I also heard her whimpering.

"Is it your chronic pain troubling you again?" I asked. "Shall I call Doctor Das?"

"No need," said my wife. "It'll go away by itself. Hoo... hiii... hooo!" she moaned.

Was it hysteria, I wondered? She didn't have that before. Perhaps yesterday's happenings upset her. She, of course, did not know of my plan. Women always wish to see the weddings arranged in a neat way. But such haste would never work out. Keshto had just swallowed the bait; it would now be awhile before we could fish him out.

In the evening, I left for Moonshine villa. I intended to talk to Keshto and calm him down. But there, I could not find Keshto; Uncle Nokur wasn't there either. The members of the young hearts' assembly were all on their beds, with a vacant look in their eyes. My queries elicited no answers from them. Perhaps they were all terribly heartbroken, I mused!

I saw Boda, Keshto's servant, and enquired after his master.

All the tiny pores on Boda's face, placed there to facilitate seeing, breathing and talking expanded simultaneously. "Babu has fled!"

"What? Your master has fled? Where to? Maybe he's run away to Bhuvan babu's home."

"Bhuvan babu has fled, his wife too, their daughters, even the horses of their daughters, and that young lady with fair skin- which was Padma, of course- has gone away too!" It meant they all had gone away. Uncle Nokur was out, finding out more. And the young hearts' club? They knew nothing, it was futile to ask anything to them.

Suddenly, my wife's strange behavior came back to my mind. I realized now, it was neither hysteria nor colic pain; she was just trying hard to suppress her laughter! I returned home at once.

"You're the root of all these happenings!" I told her.

"How? You messed up everything, now you're putting the blame on me. What's my fault?" she asked.

"So, what exactly happened? Tell me!"

At first, my wife gave out a frantic laughter, rolling on the sofa. Then, collecting her breath, she said, "You left at around ten-thirty yesterday. Tuni-didi and I chatted on, talking about our joys and sorrows. Around midnight, Keshto came into our room, looking sad, and with a mad look in his eyes. Tuni-didi wanted to know what was wrong? Keshto said he couldn't wait any longer. If he couldn't marry Padma, he'd commit suicide. It was either Padma or some acid for him! So, I said, "Don't worry. The acid is available at the doctor's chamber, and as for Padma, she's right here. Wait till morning, then we'll think of what we can do."

Keshto said, he was ready to give up his clown's appearance, and would change into an appearance suiting a gentleman. But then, after all the lofty talks he'd given on love, how could he now face the club members? Tuni didi suggested him not to worry at all. "Let's run away to Calcutta by the first train tomorrow. I'll get you married to Padma as soon as we reach there." Hearing this, Padma started a lot of fuss. But you know how Tuni didi is, nothing is impossible for her to do! She said, 'Don't behave in such an affected manner, Padma."And that very night, she got all their luggage packed, in total 163 pieces. This morning, I first saw them off at the station, before coming home.

XXXXXXX

Keshto avoided meeting me for the first one and half months after his marriage. Yesterday, he dropped by, seeking my forgiveness. I've forgiven him from the depths of my heart and I assured him that there was no need to feel embarrassed in front of me. After reading psychology,

I understood it was Keshto's sub-conscious mind that went berserk and prompted him to behave in such a preposterous manner. I found out many examples from the book to substantiate my findings.

Keshto dissolved the club. He, however, found another club, where he recruited only two members- my wife and me. The club, called *Haihoi* (Noisy, deafening, happening) club, had nothing in common with the historical Haihoi dynasty. This coming Christmas holidays, all the members plan to visit Peshawar, from Calcutta, and our sole intention is to entertain ourselves!

Jaishankar Prasad

The Beacon Light
Aakashdeep

"Prisoner!"

"What is it? Let me sleep."

"Do you wish to be free?"

"Not now. Maybe after my sleep is over. Keep quiet!"

"Such an opportunity won't come again."

"It's pretty cold. If only someone brought a blanket and saved me from the cold."

"There's a chance of storm today. This is the chance. My shackles are loose today."

"Are you then a prisoner, too?"

"Yes. Shhh.... Speak softly. In this boat, there are only ten sailors and guards."

"Will I get weapons?"

"Yes, you will. Would you be able to cut the chords attached to the ship?"

"Yes."

Lingering waves surged into the sea. The two prisoners clashed with each other. The first prisoner freed himself, and he attempted to open the fetters of the second one. As the waves crashed, both veered forwards, almost touching each other. In the impossible hope of freedom, they embraced as they came free on that dark night. The second prisoner hugged his companion in great happiness. Then, in utter surprise, he exclaimed, "What is this? Are you a woman?"

"Is it a sin to be a woman?" The woman asked, as she separated herself from his embrace.

"Where are the weapons? And your name?"

"Champa."

Between the spangled blue, star-studded firmament and the endless span of ocean, the wind raved. It played truant, as it unified with the darkness. The sea agitated violently, the waves tumultuous, and amidst them, the boat heaved. Exercising caution, the woman started rolling. As she clashed against a drunk sailor, she took away his dagger, before rolling back to the prisoner. Suddenly, the guard at the helm of the boat called out, "A storm!"

The warning bells started ringing, and everyone became alert. The prisoner lay immobile. Someone caught the rope, while the other was unfurling the mast. The prisoner somehow reached the rope that was tied to the ship. As the stars above went undercover, the waves broke and crashed without a pause. The sea now thundered and growled. A blaring storm, like a lecherous demoness, held the ship like a ball in her palm, and roared out in laughter.

In one jerky movement, the ship came free. The two prisoners giggled, despite surrounded by danger, but in the din of sorrow and darkness everywhere, no one heard them.

2

On the endless expanse of moving water, a mellifluous morning broke out, and the shimmering rays smiled brightly at the waves. The sailors saw the ship was rudderless, and the prisoners were free.

The leader asked, "Buddhagupt! Who freed you?"

Raising his dagger, Buddhagupt replied, "This one!"

The leader then said, "Wait till I capture you again."

"For whom? The captain of our ship, Mani Bhadra, is no more. He's drowned. Now, I'm the leader of this ship."

"You? Pirate Buddhagupt? Not at all."

Saying so, the leader groped for his dagger, but Champa had already seized it. Anger ran deep through him.

"Then you get ready for a duel. Whoever wins in the duel would be the captain of this ship." Saying so, Buddhagupt signed Champa to give the dagger back to the leader.

A fierce battle raged on. Both were skilled, they fought with great speed. With great dexterity, Buddhagupt freed his hands, while holding the dagger in between his teeth. As Champa looked on, astonished and afraid, the sailors enjoyed the duel. Soon, the leader's hand that held the dagger was in Buddhagupt's vice-like grip, and with a menacing call, he pushed him down. In the morning's splendor, Buddhagupt's victorious, bright dagger shone in his hands, while the leader's eyes pleaded for mercy.

Buddhagupt said, "Do you accept me as the leader now?"

"I'm just a servant, I swear upon the sea-god. I'll not betray you."

Buddhagupt spared him.

Coming closer to Buddhagupt, Champa tended to his wounds, and with her tender looks and her soft hands, she tried to relieve him of his pain. The drops of red blood now marked his beautiful body like signs of victory.

Buddhagupt rested for some time. "Where are we now?" he asked.

"Quite far from the island of Bali. We are nearing a new island. Not many people live there. The merchants from Sri Lanka frequent that island."

"When will we reach there?"

"With a favorable wind, we can be there in coming two days. Until then, we'd have no dearth of food."

Soon, the servant asked the sailors to plug a hole in the ship, and he himself began steering the boat. When Buddhagupt asked him the reason, he said, "A piece of rock lies submerged here. If we're not careful, we might hit against it."

3

"Why did they imprison you?" Buddhagupt asked Champa.

"The ship's captain, Mani Bhadra, had evil intentions about me."

"Where is your home?"

"On the bank of river *Jahnavi* (It is a tributary of river Bhagirathi), there's a city called Champa. I'm a *Kshatriya* (One of the four social orders of Hindu society, associated with the warrior class) girl," she replied. "My father used to be a guard at Mani Bhadra's place. After my mother passed away, I too lived with my father on the ship. The sea has been my home since I was eight years old. When you attacked our ship, it was my father who killed seven of your pirate friends. He died in that skirmish. Since then, I'm alone, an orphan, under this sprawling blue sky, upon the vastness of the sea. A terrible helplessness embraces me always. One day, Mani Bhadra came to me with an indecent proposal, and I sent him away, abusing him. And then, he imprisoned me."

Champa fumed with anger.

"I'm also a Kshatriya man, from *Tamralipti* (It was a city in ancient Bengal, located on the Bay of Bengal), Champa. Unfortunately, I've to find my livelihood by looting ships. I'm a pirate. What do you intend to do now?"

"I'll let my destiny take me wherever it has to. I do not wish to decide my fate." Champa's eyes looked far in the beyond, bereft of blooming-red desire, full of innocent faith. Buddhagupt, the merchant-marauder pirate, stared at her, his young, bewildered heart brimming over with respect for her. It was arousing the first feelings of youth in him. The beautiful evening danced over the sea, creating a melody of its own. Champa's unbridled hair graced her back. In the eyes of the fierce sea rover, she appeared ethereal, a young girl sparkling in her brilliance. Astonished, he fumbled around the corners of his heart, and came across a new feeling nestling there- tenderness!

Just then, the servant said, "We've reached near the island!"

The boat touched the shore. Undaunted, Champa jumped out and the sailors too embarked. Buddhagupt said, "If this is a nameless island, why don't we call it as Champa island?"

Champa laughed at hearing that.

4

After five years passed....

In the blue heavens, the autumn-stars shimmered. Moon's bright glory won in the sky, and the goddess of autumn showered the blessings of flowers.

Sitting on the high altar of Champa island, the young girl lit a lamp. With great care, she put the lamp inside the isinglass and flicked the thread with her tender fingers. The lamp rose while she watched it grow, her eyes demure and excited. It was Champa's wish that her lamp, like a beacon, reached the stars and mingle with them. However, she withdrew from the thought, knowing that it was not destined.

In front of her eyes, the silvery sparkle quivered on the sea. The sea-God Varun was busy making a garland as high as hills, extracting diamonds and sapphires from the depths of the waves. And the waves, with their bewitching laughter, rose and fell, like the deceiving desires of our heart. From afar, the banshee sound of the fisherman wafted like music through the air. On the infinite blue of water, Champa's image seemed to blur, half- formed, as if in a haze, circling to attain fulfillment. Distracted, she got up, and seeing no one near her, she called out, "Jaya!"

A dusky young tribal girl came near her. Her smile was like the pure stars, shimmering against the blue sky. She addressed Champa as her queen, as per Buddhagupt's orders.

"When will the great sailor return? Ask someone and let me know."

As Jaya left, Champa turned back. The wind, rustling across some faraway land, reached her, and wished to rest on her lap. It made her delirious, tickling her heart. A tall, well-built man walked up to her. He put his hand on her back, startling her. Champa turned and said, "Buddhagupt, it is you!"

"Are you crazy? Is this your job? Sitting here and lighting this lamp?" he asked.

"Shall I ask the maids to light the lamp, to please the gods resting on the milky seabed?" she asked in reply.

"I'm amused. Whom do you want to show the way by your beacon? Him, whom you think to be your God?"

"Indeed; for they too get lost, they too err; Or else why would they bestow so much wealth upon you, Buddhagupt?"

"What's wrong with that, Champa, the queen of this island!"

"Please free me from this prison. O skilled sailor, now you dominate the trade routes of Bali, Java, and Sumatra. But thinking back to those days when you had only one boat, and we lived on the shores of Champa, with our trade goods, still fills me with delight. Countless times our boat would dance on the sparkling waters of this sea, Buddhagupt! In that lonely timelessness, when the tired boatmen went to sleep, when the lamps would die off, and darkness surrounded us, you and I would stare at each other, our spent bodies wrapped in the mast... under the canopy of sonorous stars...."

"But Champa, we can live in a grand manner, much better than those days. You're my savior, you're everything to me."

"No, I'm not. Although you gave up being a pirate, but your heart still carries the remnants of your previous life. You're as merciless, coveting, and volatile as before. You make fun of my God, of my lamp, my beacon that I wish to light. Buddhagupt! Do you remember that stormy night when we're so worried about finding just a ray of light? I remember my father, I remember him going out in the sea, I was a child then, and my mother hanged the small, earthen lamp covered in a bamboo case on the tallest groove, on the banks of the *Bhagirathi* (It is one of the headstreams of the river Ganges). And she prayed, *My Lord! Guide my wayward sailor in the darkness, so that he may walk the right path.* And when my father returned after years, he'd say, *dear pious lady! Because of your prayers, God saved me in the hours of peril.* My mother would be beside herself with joy. Sailor, this lamp is in her memory. You're responsible for the death of my brave father. Go away!"

Rage colored her face. Buddhagupt had never seen her in such agitation.

He laughed out. "What's this, Champa? You'd be sick like this."

Saying so, he left, while Champa clenched her fist in anger.

The waves collapsed against the lonely shore, and dispersed, while a tired, orange sun glided in the western sky. In its raging, tumultuous depths, the calm sea seemed to be in deep thoughts. The fledgling sun rays on its surface seemed to distract it.

Champa and Jaya walked with unhurried steps, and stood on the shore. The wind rustled and pulled at their dresses. As Jaya signalled, there came a small boat, and they boarded on that. While Jaya rowed the boat, Champa's pensive eyes were on the sea, and she wished she could merge herself with the swelling sea.

"So much water, such coolness! But neither can I drink it, nor can it quench the thirst of my heart. So, what should I do? Should I cry, just as the waves wail, drifting away from the shore? Or should I merge with the sea, like that golden-orb in the sky?" The inflamed sun resembled a ball of pain. Before her eyes, it dipped to the depths of the sea. With a deep sigh, Champa turned away her face from the sight. There, near her, on another boat was Buddhagupt. He lent his hands towards her. Holding it, she came on his boat and sat next to him.

"It's unsafe to row in such a small boat," he said. "You know, there's that submerged rock somewhere nearby. Your boat could have struck against that..."

"It'd be better to be imprisoned in the depths of water, than be your prisoner, within these high walls..."

"Oh, how heartless you are, Champa! Just order me once, what wouldn't I do for you! I can create a new island for you, bring subjects for you, create a new kingdom for you.... just give me a chance, test me, if you wish to! If you say, I'm ready to scrape my heart out with this dagger, and let it drown in the depths of this mighty ocean." The powerful sailor, whose name reigned supreme through the lands of Bali, Java, and Champa, the one who challenged the roaring winds, sat on his knees before her, his eyes brimming with tears.

The green ranges of the hills nearby stood in awe of the tanned evening dawning on the rippling sea. Nature was creating a dream-like place of rest with her compassionate thoughts. Like an enchantress, she was birthing a phantasmagoria, drenching the entire space with ambrosia, filling the universe with blue lotuses. Maddened, lost in their fragrance, Champa held Buddhagupt's hands in hers. She embraced him. Almost in an intimate embrace between the earth and the sea. As soon as reality dawned on her, she drew out the dagger from her blouse.

"Buddhagupt, today I'll relinquish this dagger of revenge into the heart of the sea. My heart has always betrayed me, again and again."

The bright dagger flashed and disappeared, tearing the heart of the grating sea.

"Shall I trust now that I've your forgiveness, that you've forgiven me?" Deeply surprised, the splendid sailor asked, his voice trembling.

"Trust? No, no, Buddhagupt. I cannot trust my heart; it has betrayed me; then how do I trust you? I hate you, and yet I can die for you! I love you."

Champa cried as she uttered those words. The vibrant evening of colors was almost closing its eyes as dusk fell. Drawing a deep sigh, the sailor said, "In the memory of this sacred moment in my life, I'll build a lighthouse here, Champa! Here, on this hill. Perhaps the blurred evening of my life shall be brightened with its light."

5

In the distant part of the island, there rose a range of small hills. For the greater part, it stood submerged in the sea, and the perky, frisky waves crashed on it, cloaked it in secrecy. The ancient tribes on the island had assembled there today, celebrating a festival. They came together to adorn Champa in the robes of the forest goddess. The soldiers from Tamralipti carried Champa, dressed as the *Devi*, a goddess, in a palanquin.

On the highest peak of the hill, a lighthouse stood, intending to warn the sailors of impending dangers. The tribal group were celebrating the inaugural moment of the lighthouse. Buddhagupt, who stood at the gate of the lighthouse, extended his arm to Champa, helping her step out of the palanquin. As they together entered inside the lighthouse, strains of the flute and the beats of the drum wafted in. The forest girls, dressed in mesmerizing flower ornaments, sprinkled flowers on them, and their dance started.

Watching them from atop the light house, Champa asked Jaya, "Oh, how nice! Where are those girls coming from?"

"It is the queen's wedding today," said Jaya, and she smiled at her.

Buddhagupt's eyes stared out at the sea. Shaking him up, Champa asked, "Is it the truth?"

"If your heart desires it, we can wed Champa. It is now for ages that I carry this inflamed desire, like a volcano, in my heart."

"Shut up, sailor! Are you trying to take advantage of my helpless situation like this?"

"Champa, I'm not the killer who killed your father. Some other pirate killed him!"

"If only I could trust you! Buddhagupt, it would indeed be a moment sublime, a moment most desired! Even in your cruelty, you'd have been an epitome of greatness for me."

Jaya had already left them alone, sitting side by side, in that narrow chamber.

Buddhagupt now held Champa's feet in his own hands. His voice throbbing with passion, he said, "Champa, we have been so far away from our motherland, India, and here, amidst these innocent tribal people, we're worshipped like *Indra and Sachi* (The king of the gods and his wife in Hinduism). I often remember that land of philosophers. I often think back to the glory of that land. The memories beckon me, and yet, why don't I return there? Despite all the greatness thrust upon me, I'm still a pauper at heart. The day you touched that hardened heart of mine, it glowed like a precious stone. I'm an atheist Champa! I don't believe in God, neither in sin, nor in mercy. It is difficult for me to make sense of the afterlife. But I trust a part of my enfeebled heart. I respect its feelings. Like an unknown star, you shine on my empty horizon, smiling like a ray of light on my darkest destiny. My mind, once the admirer and worshipper of wealth, now craves solitude for happiness. Would you come with me? Would you like to travel back, like a queen, to our motherland, with ships laden with endless wealth? Let us get married today, let us then leave for India tomorrow. Even the mighty waves listen to this sailor's command, and they would sail our ship away, like the southerly wind, to the shores of India. Come Champa, let us go!"

Coming closer, Champa held his hand in hers. Trembling, they came closer, their lips sealed in union. But only for a while; for soon, reality dawned upon Champa. "Buddhagupt! For me, the land is just soil, and all water is mere liquid. For me, each breeze of wind is cooling. My heart is not ablaze with any special desire. My dear sailor, go back to your motherland, enjoy the riches, the wealth you've accumulated. Leave me here, amidst these innocent tribal people, to look after them, to care for their sorrows."

"I'll for sure leave then, Champa; for staying here, near you, I'd perhaps be unable to control myself! Ah, I wish I drown in those waves!" He cried out in a despondent voice. "What would you do here, alone?"

"I wished to light the lamp in this lighthouse, as a mark of respect for my father. Now I realize that I too perhaps must burn here, like the beacon."

One golden morning, from her lighthouse, Champa observed a row of ships, leaving the shore, sailing towards the northwest expanse of water. Her eyes teared.

This is a tale dating back to several centuries. Champa lit the lamp, her beacon, as long as she lived in that lighthouse. And when she passed away, the inhabitants of the island, for years, paid respect to that kind-hearted, gentle soul worshipping her almost like a goddess.

But then, one day, Time, with its hardened hands, broke it down from its elevated stand.

Jaishankar Prasad

In Charity
Bheekh mein

Brajraj was absorbed in conversation as he sat on the brick verandah, on a blanket with Minna. In the pond nearby, the lotuses bloomed, and a slow, fragrant breeze wafted through them towards the cottage.

"Ma was saying..." Minna said, as he scattered the petals of the lotus.

"What was she saying?"

"Your father will go abroad. He will bring a Nepali pony for you."

"Are you going to ride on a pony, or on a horse, you crazy boy!"

"No, I shall ride on a pony. It doesn't fall."

"Then I'll not go."

"Why won't you go? Hu... Hu... Hu... I'll start crying now."

"All right, tell me, when you earn, what will you get for us?"

"A lot of money." Saying so, Minna raised up his small hands, as high as he could.

"You will give all the money to me, right?"

"No, I'll give to Ma as well."

"How much shall you give to me?"

"A bagful."

"And to your mother?"

"As much as can fit into the wooden box."

"All right, then ask you mother to get the Nepali pony for you."

Irritated, Minna climbed on Brajraj's shoulders and turned him into a pony. Peeking out from the interiors, Indo watched the fun and frolic between the father and the son. She said, "Minna, this one is a stubborn pony."

This ridicule irritated Brajraj. Indo had already reprimanded him that morning. Enacting her wifely position at home, Indo would speak disagreeably with him, and her harsh words would leave him feeling pessimistic and skeptical. He felt so complete in this world by just playing, arguing, and then reconciling with Minna that he found it utterly meaningless to do anything else. They were not in a starving position, but it did not satisfy Indo. As she watched her idle husband engage in flirting with Malo, she felt jealous. Brajraj would understand everything, but he disregarded it. He was quite happy with Minna in their bricked cottage, but that day he felt irked.

"Minna, at times the stubborn ponies run, and then they do not stop without bothering about the path. Your mother dominates over the house and over her soaked chickpeas. What if this pony gets attracted to the taste of fresh and green grass? "

"No Minna! People who are satisfied with just whatever they have, they will never do that."

"They can do it, Minna. Just tell her that…"

Minna grew anxious. This was a novel manner of

communication. He could not understand it. He said, "Yes, they can do it."

"I know well what they can do!" Saying so, Indo closed the door with a bang, and went inside. Frustration flashed hard in Brajraj's bosom. Hate flared up, almost like lightning. He turned skeptical of his own existence. Was he a man or not? Such lashing words! How doubting she was always. His mind was in a revolting state. All this while, he had trained his mind, like an astute moneylender, to augment the principle. He could never diminish this burden by accepting the affections of Indo. But now, at that very moment, he opened his bag of frustration to recover every insult with compound interest.

He cradled Minna once in his lap, and then as evening fell, people started returning to their home, carrying the ploughs on their shoulders. He left home.

A retired Sikh pensioner was running a bus on the route between Jalandhar to Jwalamukhi. His bus driver was a smart man trained in Kolkata. The simpletons in the village were very excited by this occurrence. All those who had promised the goddess a visit for several years, but only postponed their trip because of the impending arduous journey by the bullock carts, now got ready to visit the shrine, full of excitement.

In the bus, women wearing beautiful scarves, embroidered shawls, nice stitched shalwars, now came frequently. But the driver was only engrossed with the machine. He had no eyes for any of them. He seemed in love with only the horn, brakes, and mudguards. Holding the steering in his hands, when he drove his bus through that verdant valley of green, his focus never wavered from the road ahead. His possessions included a long coat, a blanket, and a globular, round vessel to carry water. And, of course, from time to time, with the small amount of money that he saved, he dropped into the concealed box under the seat. He did not wish to see the wild creepers of rose winding around the tall trees on the mountain top. Their crisp, sweet fragrance unfolded and spread across, rousing him deeply. But he forced himself to focus back on his bus and concentrated on driving it through the less frequented paths. Many years passed in this manner.

The old Sikh was happy to hire him. His driver neither smoked nor used tobacco and never wasted money.

That day, the clouds spilled over the overcast sky. It also brought in some drizzling rain. His bus tore through the middle of the lonely street amidst the valley. He would pass by a few villages comprising two or three homes. His bus was not crowded. A family whom the Sikh pensioner was familiar with was on their journey to the shrine in *Jwalamukhi* (It is a famous temple to the goddess of the flaming face in the valley of Kangra in Himachal Pradesh). They had hired the bus, but as of now the driver did not feel it necessary to know how many of them had boarded the bus. As soon as he realized the engine needed water, he stopped the bus. Taking the bucket, Brajraj went to fetch water. The passengers on the bus started feeling thirsty, and the old Sikh said, "Brajraj! Please give some water to them as well."

As he approached the passengers with the bucket of water, he felt that the beautiful woman who extended the water vessel to him looked familiar. It distracted him, as he poured water on her vessel, and some of the water spilled over on her stole. The passenger responded in an irritated manner. "Look out!"

The lady looked at him from the corner of her eyes. In

her ears, the name 'Brajraj' also kept ringing. Brajraj went back to his seat.

The old Sikh and the passenger both found his behavior rather indecent, but they refrained from commenting. The bus started moving. Like a film in motion, the scenic beauty of the valley of Kangra kept changing. But before Brajraj's eyes, different images flashed through......

The village pond, where lotuses bloomed, rippled like the pure love of Minna. In that love, there was the longing to attain peace. In between, how Malti rattled her thick silver toe rings on seeing him, and how his wife, in a spree of suspicion, would send him to go out of home. She also snatched away the love of his life, the love that he received from his son. There was a reason behind this. Indo believed Brajraj was in love with Maalo-she was the only beautiful, and cheerful girl who was yet unmarried in their village. That was Maalo... and now this woman in stole, all dressed up like a Punjabi lady? Was that possible? Indeed, it was her---Maalo! Holding the steering wheel in his hands, he still wanted to have another look at her, just to be sure of his memory. It was her face that brought back so many forgotten memories. Unable to resist himself, he turned back to have one more look at her.

The bus crashed against a tree. And although it caused minor damage, nor was anyone injured, it irritated the Sikh. Brajraj never sat behind the wheel after that. His boss did not tolerate this petty lapse by him. Nobody had any compassion for the other. Brajraj left the job.

Not that Brajraj lived a life of complete detachment. But his life as a householder did not take off well. There was a lack of happiness in his simple married life. It was only the childish talks of Minna and Malti's delightful flirting that provided the aroma of fresh lemon juice in the bland *sherbet* that his life was.

When he lost that, he stayed back in Calcutta, and took the training to be a driver. Amidst the hills and the valleys, he found some peace. The small villages, comprising a couple of houses, filled his mind with detached fondness. Sitting on his bus, he would cast a glance of indifference at the faraway houses and drive past them. It was his way of taking revenge upon his own village. But ever since he left his job as a driver of the bus, he changed a lot. He started living in the precincts where the priests lived, near Jwalamukhi.

He started spending the savings he had with him. As days passed, the peace in his mind and the strength in his body declined. If someone requested him, he did the chore for him, but he would not accept any money in return. People thought him to be a man of gold. There were many who befriended him. He had no thoughts about his own home, his own life, and spent his days like this. Of course, he tried hard to forget. But Minna? Then he thought, 'He must have grown up now, the one who forced me to leave home, and go away seeking work. She must have raised him up well. They must have managed with what came from farming. I was the only surplus person in the household. And Malti? No, at first, Indo threw me away from home, for she suspected me with Malti. And then, the moment I remembered Malti, I lost my job. I don't know what made me think about her. What would she do here in Punjab? I shouldn't even take her name! Indo must be thrilled to get rid of me!'

However, his intoxication lasted only for a few years. The most important resource in this materialistic age ran out. He was, by now, a pauper, forced to beg. His mindset changed, too. He wouldn't find a job, but he would run errands for others. He was now ready to accept money in exchange.

That morning, he woke up early and sat near the temple. In his heart, a flame raged for a while before snuffing out. But there was no one who glanced in his way, although there were hordes of travelers walking past.

It was the month of *Chaitra* (first month of the Hindu calendar) and there were many visitors. Brajraj too extended his palm to beg from them. A gentleman, carrying a child in his arm, walked past him, while a woman paused for a while as she adjusted her stole. Women are tender-hearted souls. As his mind prompted these words, Brajraj supplicated before the lady, not wishing to be turned away empty-handed at his first attempt.

She stopped. "Don't you drive the bus anymore?"

Oh, she sounded exactly like Malti!

Folding his palms away, Brajraj asked, "Who are you? Maalo?"

"And you're Brajraj, right?"

Taking a deep breath, he replied, "Yes, I am."

Malti kept standing. "Do you beg these days?"

"Yes, earlier I begged for happiness. I begged for a bit of tenderness from Minna, love from Indo, for a doable produce from my small farmland, and I begged for some friendly remarks from my so-called friends. I tried to tie these up in a small bundle to be happy. Like a mendicant, I am now living far away, removed from everyone, in isolation, clinging to that happiness. Your presence is like the sprinkling of pleasure on me..."

"Indo has been quite crazy! She started suspecting me. After you left, she came twice to fight with me. But now I've come here..." Saying so, she looked fearfully after the gentleman who had just passed Brajraj by.

"Is that your boy?"

"Yes," said Maalo. She brought out something to give it to him.

Brajraj said, "You go, Maalo. Look, your husband is coming this way."

Carrying the child in his arm, her husband walked back to them. Malti seemed angry, withdrawn, and restless now. Emotions of anxiety, fear and curious compassion flitted across her face.

"Is that beggar troubling you?" her husband asked in a scolding voice.

Turning towards the priest, Maalo's husband asked, "Why do you all allow such rogues here?"

How could the priest tolerate the insult of a rich client! Dragging Brajraj by the arm, he said, "Get up. If I ever see you loitering here again, I shall make sure that you lose your leg."

As he was being pushed and shoved, Brajraj thought, *"It is Malti yet again! Have I ever asked her for anything? It is my misfortune. Even though I did not seek for it, that is what she has been giving to me! Today, on my very first day of begging, too, she gave me the same misfortune in the name of charity..."*

Bibhutibhushan Bandopadhyay

The Atheist
Nastik

When Loknath's studies were over, he went to his master to bid goodbye to him. The master decreed then that he must always remember that his name was Loknath- that meant 'lord of all worlds', that he was 'above all other men'. He blessed Loknath that he may fulfil the meaning of his name in his life and attain success.

Loknath was his brightest, most favorite, and most intelligent student. Bidding him farewell, the master fell silent for quite some days.

After leaving his master's school, Loknath did not approach any royal court. He showed no interest in teaching either. Nor was he keen on getting married and settling down. For a while, he roamed around in a wayward manner. At last, he came beside the *Punyabhadra* river, built himself a small hut, and started living there. Most of the people, therefore, took him to be mad.

Ever since his childhood days, Loknath differed from the rest. On the days when the sun brought forth abundant brightness, he'd roam alone in the village field, all alone. He'd not mix with the boys of his own age. Late in the evening, when the small, distant hill would look like a huge chunk of cloud, fallen off from the cloud above, Loknath would sit under the greying sky, in the field near the edge of the forest. He would fix his childish gaze upon that hill. For hours altogether, deep thoughts would preoccupy him. He believed, in his childlike mind, that hill on the horizon was the last point on earth, that the earth ended there. *'And if I pass that hill, and go further away, far away, even far away, and yet further away, where would I reach then?'* His boyish mind would stagger at the very thought of crossing the familiar boundary, and reach that yet unknown, imaginary world. He'd forget the thoughts of his own home and even his siblings. Under the hazy light of the impending dusk, he would sit, his mind engrossed in visualizing the distant, silent land beyond the ever-changing clouds. In that land, he believed, the fight between Ram and Ravan still lingered on, and the headless demon was still groping in the darkness, much in the same way as the tales of Ramayana and Mahabharat, which he heard from his grandma. It would be the amazing land of bizarre things.

But those days were long over. Growing up, Loknath turned into a very harsh and hard-hearted person. His appearance, to match up with his arid erudition, turned crude and inelegant. With the lengthy, unkempt hair on his enormous head, along with his rough beard flying in the air, he appeared rather terrible. His eyes would flash with a sharp, steely look of intellect; but at times, the look in his eyes calmed down, and he'd look composed, handsome, and noble.

The sweeping thirst for the distant that Loknath had in his childhood started exposing itself as he grew older. Before turning thirty, his mind started questioning everything that was visible in this universe. The ludicrous question of whether there was a supreme creator in this universe puzzled and frustrated him a lot. His goals, too, appeared to be rather strange to the ordinary people. He looked down upon the human efforts to gain material gain and comfort; the idea of attaining fame and name too had no significance in his eyes. Once, the teacher in the seminary received a letter from the city of *Magadha*, (A region and one of the sixteen great kingdoms (600-200 BCE) now in South Bihar, India) seeking a senior advisor for the Royal court. The court had lost their chief counsellor, and the post felt vacant at his demise. The teacher selected Loknath. He wanted to send him to the court with due respect, pomp, and show. But Loknath refused his proposal right away and sent one of his friends instead. Soon after this, he left the seminary, and within a year, took shelter beside the secluded bank of Punyabhadra.

For thirty years now, Loknath had been living alone in the small hut. He received twice a year food grains and two garments from the Jain religious community. Wild cotton grew in the fields nearby his hut, and he'd himself make any other garment, if required, using this cotton. In the beginning, he'd started giving lessons to a couple of students. Soon he gained an excellent reputation as a teacher, and students flocked to him, owing to his elevated character and intellect. Frustrated, he then completely stopped teaching.

The banks of Punyabhadra, in those days, had lush, deep forests on both sides. In some parts of the higher mountains, there grew *Sal* and *deodar* trees. There were thorny bushes and creeping vines in the lower altitudes. Loknath's house stood under the shade of these dense trees, where the narrow stream of the river divided the valley and went to the other side of the mountain.

Loknath's hut was special, housing a collection of handwritten manuscripts. He wrote on wide-ranging topics on *Vedas, Smritis, Upanishads, Puranas,* on works of Panini (He was a Sanskrit philologist, grammarian who gave a detailed description of Sanskrit Grammar) and other masters of grammar, and on the works of the ancient astrologers. In great detail, he penned his works on the leaves of *taal* and *bhurja* leaves (White, paper like barks used for writing Sanskrit texts in ancient India) and placed them between the wooden book covers he made of two pieces of thin layered wood. These books and many others lay piled up and scattered on his floor, making it almost impossible to step inside there.

Each day, early in the morning, after taking a bath, Loknath would sit under the shade of the old *neem* tree before his hut and read the books with full attention.

On some lazy afternoons, when the warm wind wafted the fresh fragrance of the blooming *neem* flowers, Loknath's mind produced a dream-like vision. In that space, the snow haired *Aryabhatta* (He was the first major mathematician from the classical age of Indian mathematics. He gave the world the digit "0") would trace chalk lines against a vast blue sky, explaining the position of the stars and planets to his disciple *Shakatayan*. Amidst the inexhaustible clamoring of the flock of wild birds, *Yaska* (He was an early Sanskrit grammarian) would discuss his theories on languages. And *Parashar*, the maharishi, faced with the challenging geometrical theorem, would stare with a deep frown at the anthill before his eyes. Startled, Loknath would come to his senses then. It would dawn upon him he has been, until now, visualizing Yaska's face reflected on the wild swans' swimming on river.

Observing the stars at night, Loknath would wonder

what they were. He did not find much help from the texts written by the ancient astronomers. After deep thoughts, he himself concluded that the cluster of stars were nothing but a kind of enormous masses of radiant crystals, placed in the universe to provide light. He considered the moon to be a larger mass of crystal. He recorded his viewpoints on stars and planets in a manuscript which were discovered after his death. About the source of light, Loknath wrote the crystals found in the space were of much superior quality than those found on earth, and hence they emanated an innate light. His writings contained many of his scientific analysis, geometrical drawings, and although these proved that he was a talented scientist of exceptional qualities, he was neither averse to criticism, nor unwelcoming of other viewpoints. What he disliked was being mediocre. For him, it had to be the pinnacle of knowledge or mere ignorance. He discarded anything in between.

Once, after intense hard work, he wrote a treatise on *Samkhya* (The Samkhya is the oldest of all the Indian philosophical systems. It is the first known description of a complete model of the universe). After finishing the thesis, he felt it was far below his expectation. It contained many flaws, and despite repeated attempts, Loknath could not correct them the way he wished. One morning, carrying the manuscript in his hand, he walked to the banks of the Punyabhadra river. The reeds trembled in the faint breeze of the morning. Loknath threw away the manuscript that he gave shape to after years of grueling hard work. In a moment, the script sank in the rippling waters, like a piece of stone. It only startled the feeble waves with this sudden immersion as they encountered the intense erudition *Samkhya* captured in those scriptures!

With passaging time, Loknath became restless. It

was now impossible for him to sit in one place for long. He was losing his mental peace. There were days when he ate almost nothing, and spent the day roaming on the banks of the river, like an alarmed person. He wouldn't stare at the stars at night anymore; and, if he did, he'd cover his eyes at once with his two hands and look downwards in guilt. He'd be very much like that school student who had not completed his task and was reprimanded by the blinking stars through the torn clouds. At night, in the stillness of the forest, thousands of questions would surround him. And he'd wonder in desperation: why couldn't the *Vedas* or the *Upasargas* (A term used in Sanskrit grammar to explain a special class of prepositional particles) offer any answers to these questions?

It brought him back to the scriptures again, and he concentrated on the philosophical writings. However, reading them increased his displeasure, and that reflected on his face. On reading the ways of attaining happiness as devised by the philosophers increased his frustration. Within the folds of his books, at night, *Patanjali* (He was an Indian scholar and philosopher, probably from the 2nd century BC, whose name is traditionally associated with the Yoga Sutras) would cast a sarcastic eye towards *Gautam* (A great sage in Hinduism), while rishi *Kapil* (A great Hindu sage) would give an arrogant stare at *Jaimini* (An ancient Indian scholar), and *Vyas deva* (A legendary sage, regarded to be the compiler of the Hindu epic Mahabharata) continued to shrink in gloom within the pages, fearing to be ranked with these fools! Fatigued, when Loknath retired to bed after his studies at night, he felt as if there was a war raging inside his dark hut, where the philosophers, instead of lending each other a listening ear, were engaged in a verbal fight. The translators and the illustrators were almost at each other's throat, piling words upon heaps of words. Sleep deserted him, and the ancient smell of the dried leaves of the scriptures stifled his breath.

Rushing out of his hut, he would come out and stand under the neem tree. Some days, the forest beyond would look uncanny under the slice of moon. And on some days, the frightful chorus of the night insects stirred through the solid veil of darkness. The cluster of glow worms shone through the brambles. The cool night breeze would soothe him. But only for a while. For, soon enough, the questions rushed back at him, tearing through the darkness like some macabre specter. If God created light, then was there also a creator who created this darkness? If absence of light defined darkness, was darkness then a self-defined state? Was it then self-sprung? Did it exist prior to the creation?

Slowly, Loknath would go back to his hut, rekindle his lamp, and, taking up the scriptures, he would once again seek the answers. There were days when he would not study at all. Sitting in silence, his eyes would stare at the sky. His mind, in a restless state, tried to solve the eternal puzzle, the mystery of the Creation, but the more he studied, the further he became from the prospect of reaching the answers. He seemed caught amidst darkness without a ray of light.

Even a couple of years back, Loknath believed that perhaps an enlightened sage, in those ancient ages, must have been able to find the answers to the deep mysterious questions about the origin of life and creation. For posterity, therefore, those wise sages wrote their findings with hopeful words. Loknath reminisced about the day when he had, for the very first time, found a clue to those questions in the dried, ancient text of the *Upanishads*. It happened almost twenty years ago.

A rainy night it was, still, quiet night when the lonely wind howled through the fields. Sitting in his dimly lit hut, alone, he read those words, and for a moment he trembled, as if stung by a snake bite. And closing the scripture, when he stared out, he felt that the entire creation out there, the trees, the forests, the grass, the river, trembled like him. The memory of the day brought a smile to his lips. How naïve he had been then, he thought, how unformed were his emotions! His present wiser mind cast an endearing look at his former immature self. Human mind always found it difficult to go beyond the preset boundary. And the one who claimed to know everything is a fraud, or is self-deceptive, because such a person didn't even know for what he needed to seek understanding.

His eyes travelled to the distant hills, where the new, red blossoms of *Palash* flourished in the first breath of spring.

It happened many years ago, when Loknath was twenty-one years old.

"It's nothing, dear Maya. I'll return within seven years. It won't take longer than that to finish my studies. Besides, would I be able to stay away from you for much longer?"

Blushing, seventeen-year-old Maya had said, with a smile, "Just seven years? That's not that long."

His voice brimming with deep passion, Loknath said, "Exactly my thoughts." Then, with his eyes full of trust, looking at Maya, he asked, "It is not that long for us, is it?"

Hiding her smile, Maya said, "No, it isn't. It would pass just as morning passes into evening!" And she burst out laughing.

Hesitant, a bit taken aback, Loknath said, "No, listen Maya... I wanted to say..."

In Loknath's wise, aged heart, there was no place anymore for Maya. The same Maya, who had once encouraged him to take steps towards his future, and in secrecy, had wiped away her tears. But now, at the crossroad of his life, Loknath had no time, no inclination for such trivial emotions.

While he was still studying in the seminary, his heart started undergoing a change. He not only forgot Maya, but he also learned to grow a distaste for the material comforts and pleasure in life. The thoughts of scholars, sages and philosophers then frequented his life. It was a different world, and a big, mysterious philosopher inhabited the entire expanse of his mind. Pitted against him, Maya did not stand a chance. Only fools found solace in such insignificant things, because in the depths of their hearts, the eternal query never found place.

Yet, in some careless, unguarded moment, the memories preyed upon him, like the nightly visit of the demons, hell bent on ruining the religious oblation. It took him back when he was a youth of twenty years, and Maya's demure smile, the first love of his life, had soothed him.

While he was still in the seminary, he'd heard vague rumors about Maya. She did not marry. She accepted the life of a nun entering a seminary. That too had happened long back. He had no disposition to follow the news further; he cared nothing for her.

The shadows of the evening lengthened as darkness descended around him. Walking towards his hut, Loknath looked up at the sky, and prayed, "O invisible force! I'm Loknath, the philosopher. My thinking is not like those simple, imbecilic, ordinary people. I want to know what is the reason that this visible universe exists? Does there really exist someone whom the common people refer to as

God? I've no belief in the scriptures, as I can hardly trust the veracity of the proofs they offer. I need proof from you. If you can hear my plea, please send me answers. Please do not distract me, for those shall not satisfy me."

In the seminary, there lived the esteemed philosopher Madhabacharya. Loknath went to him and put forward his questions to him. The philosopher started explaining about liberation, the various forms of liberation, the difference between liberation and salvation. Listening to his deep discourse, Loknath grew impatient and decided that he understood at least one way of liberation, and that included his liberation from the complicated rhetoric of Madhabacharya!

One day, while bathing, he felt something touching his back. Thinking it to be the tail of some animal, he at once turned back. He dipped his hand in the flowing water, and realized that it wasn't the tail of any animal, but the branch of a creeper plant growing in the water. Extracting it out of water, he saw it was a common, aquatic plant that grew in the mossy waters. Watching it, now he saw that the lower limb of the creeper- which had tickled his skin- had leaves that resembled the fir trees, but the leaves on that same creeper which floated above water were large as the leaves of betel plants. These leaves stayed exposed to sunlight, and the large size of the leaves enabled them to stay afloat on water. But had the lower part of the creeper that remained submerged in water, been equally large, the currents would have torn and washed its size away underneath. The hair-thin fir like growth on the lower portion of the creeper made it easy for the water to flow through, and it allowed the plant to survive.

The creeper and its creation made Loknath think. Finishing his bath, he walked back home, his mind full of thoughts, registering that perhaps he had found a clue about nature's creation.

His mind impressed upon him the fact that the existence of two varied types of leaves on the same creeper must be the manifestation of Nature's consciousness. Otherwise, why such a trifling object like a creeper would have such an intricate design to facilitate its survival? Who crafted the fir like branches on the same creeper so that it may survive under water?

A thought flashed through his mind. A few days back, in a restless state, he had prayed to the Almighty to provide him with a proof of His existence. Was He responding to his prayers in this fashion?

However, he quickly rejected such a thought as his logical mind found it to be too vague to be true. Reaching so quickly to a conclusion was against his nature; such a thing was only suitable for common minds. Yet, the thought kept him preoccupied as days passed. He couldn't concentrate on reading. Most of his time went in searching for something unknown beside the riverbank where the wild reeds, or the wildflowers grew in plenty, covering the water. His time passed in searching through the nests of the water birds who kept their eggs hidden under the huge leaves of the trees beside the river. Picking up the small wildflowers that grew in an array before his hut, he attentively tried to find similarities in their design and structure. He discovered each one of them had five petals surrounding one central dot. In that sprawling field, perhaps millions of flowers bloomed. Loknath picked them randomly to examine and found the same design repeating in each of the flowers: five petals surrounding one central dot.

Like a disease permeating through his body, his thirst for learning grew in leaps and bounds. Millions of questions rattled his mind, and grew huge there, like demons, and he prayed to the Almighty to fill him up with wisdom. But soon the questions distressed him immensely. He felt to be confined in a large, dark, mysterious universe with only a thin ray of light that raised his hopes. But he was desperate. His heart hankered to know the complete truth. Sleepless, the nights passed, and with his eyes raised to the night sky, he'd pray to the Creator to bless him with profound wisdom and consciousness.

While his mind was in this turmoil, one day he saw a larger insect, injecting a secretion from its body to a tiny insect, and killing it. Taking the larger insect on his palm, Loknath noticed a sharp needle like organ on it. This syringe like organ helped the insect to transfer the poison secreting from his body, through a hollow part on its body. It was amazing, this well-devised manner of killing one's victim.

Darkness clouded Loknath's mind; a tactful arrangement to kill and destroy cruelly. A ruthless God the Creator was, he felt; only the fools would call Him merciful.

The spring days and the days of autumn passed in the same manner. One day, something happened that put an end to Loknath's pain, restlessness, and constant doubt.

The monsoon was round the corner. After a long dry spell, the grass on the fields had turned arid and colorless. The wind felt as hot as the flames of fire. Towards the evening, the wind blew hard and soon, dark clouds appeared in the corners of the sky. Lying amidst the tall grasses next to the river bend, Loknath was observing the way the clouds were piling up to bring in the rains. Suddenly, he sensed something biting him between his index and middle finger. Disengaging his hand, he turned and saw the head of a poisonous snake poised to strike him once more. Without thinking, Loknath made a dash to grab its tail. Instead, his hands extracted a bunch of grass. The viper disappeared between them.

Quickly tearing strips of his clothing, he tied it around his wrist and arm, as tightly as he could, but it turned out to be rather sloppy. His mind prompted him the medicines against snake bite- the roots of the white crown flower, *Akand*a (A poisonous plant with milky, latex like secretion) and he went searching for it, but in vain. Soon his arm felt weak and numb. The venom was reaching up, he realized, and he frantically began searching through the places. He also tried to remember other medicinal herbs- the seeds of the Kusum flowers, the bark of the red sandalwood tree- but not even one was available to him. After a while, he felt dizzy, and he fell to the ground near a bush. The poison now coursed through his body.

Slowly, a brightness covered the innermost corner of his consciousness. Death was near, and yet its harsh, burning tune was being suppressed by a melody emanating from a distant, rhythmic stream that broke free of its confinement. The strain reached his ears, as if promising to free him from his prison, bless him with wisdom...

Oh, Master of the Infinite! While residing in the distant, eternal space, sitting on your throne of light, your eyes were always upon this insignificant human. Is that why you brought the water plant before my eyes, as if to give me a clue? That day, I didn't recognize you. I didn't perceive your path. Today, I understand.... I know now that you're there within my soul, greater than this universe, this heaven, pervading all that there is in this universe. Just as the cloud sustained the plants, so are you the provider of my sustenance. Does the anguish of my soul not reach you? Well then, show me the path, dear Master, take me beyond this dark kingdom, beyond the faraway horizon, beyond the end of this sea of my life, where I can glimpse Your infinite glory, your absolute knowledge that is triumphant in its depth...

The logical mind of Loknath raised its head up all at once. "You're losing your mind; you're losing your thinking power. The poison in your body is numbing your senses, preventing you from clear thinking. It is weakening you. Get rid of these weak, rambling thoughts."

Loknath's mind gave up. It was too exhausted to fight any longer. The effects of venom in his blood increased, like opium, and he slipped into the arms of sleep more definitely.

At the edge of a nameless village, somewhere faraway, two small children were picking up dates from under the wild date trees. Through the stony window of Time, their footsteps gradually faded away, as their presence grew dimmer.

From a honey flower tree in the forest, a boy and a girl are plucking honey flowers and tasting the juice. The girl is giving the juicy flower to the boy, she says- *here, try this one out, these flowers are sweeter.*

In the blue nothingness above, white bearded, radiant looking sages are going somewhere. One of them calls out to his friends, 'Dear friends, let us throw away the old water that we're carrying in our water pots, and replenish it with the fresh water of the fountain. After a long walk, we've reached the source of sweet water.' And from their water pots, a dark, inky liquid poured out.

On a cloudy evening, on a roadside, someone had beaten a girl. Her disheveled hair flew all around her face, her clothes were torn. And in a sobbing voice, she says, 'Why are you beating me, just because I came to your neighborhood? I'll never come again.... never again...'

Loknath's dying eyes fell upon the vast universe, staring at it stupefied, much like his inexperienced eyes which had gaped at it, as a child. Now the almost darkening world, garbed as an enormous question mark, peered at his face. It offered no answer to him.

Saadat Hasan Manto

TEN RUPEES
Dus Rupay

She was playing with the small girls at the corner of the narrow alley, and her mother was searching for her in the *chali*, that big house which had many floors and several small rooms. She had asked Kishori to wait in her inner apartment, and after ordering the tea-boy to bring some tea or coffee, she had already searched for her daughter on the three floors of the building. But she could not find her. She walked to the open toilet, calling out for her. 'Sarita, o Sarita!' But Sarita was nowhere to be found in the building. Her mother's suspicion was correct. After getting over the bout of dysentery, without having to use any medicine, she was playing with the small girls at the corner of the alley, where garbage lay piled up. And she was oblivious to any worry.

However, Sarita's mother seemed worried. Kishori was sitting inside. He had already informed that two wealthy businessmen were waiting with their car in the enormous market, but Sarita was nowhere to be found. Sarita's mother knew very well that it wasn't every day that rich people with cars showed up. She felt grateful to Kishori, who brought wealthy customers once or twice a month. Else, it was unthinkable of rich men to come to a filthy neighborhood as theirs, that reeked of rotting betel leaves and burnt-out *bidis*, (thin cigarettes filled with tobacco flakes) a grimy place which bothered even Kishori. He was a clever man. He never brought the customers home, but he took a decked up Sarita outside to them. To his customers, he would say, "Sir, days are pretty bad. The police are on the lookout to arrest someone. They have already caught two hundred girls. I too have a case running against me in the court. We all need to be extra careful."

Sarita's mother looked annoyed. As she took the stairs down, she saw Ram Dui sitting there, cutting the bidi leaves. She asked her, "Have you seen Sarita? I can't find her anywhere. If I find her today, I'll smack her so hard that she'd turn into a pulp. She's not a child anymore, but she runs around with those useless boys for the whole day!"

With no response, Ram Dui continued cutting the *bidi* leaves. Fact was, Sarita's mother was only muttering to herself, and Ram Dui was used to listening to that. Every third or fourth day she would go around searching for Sarita. And each time, she would gabble these very words to Ram Dui, who sat for the whole day near the stairs with her basket, tying the red and white threads to the *bidis*.

Besides this complain, she would also tell the other women in the building about her wish to get her daughter Sarita married to a rich gentleman. "That is why I insist she should study. I am thinking of enrolling her in that government school the Municipality has opened nearby in our locality. It was her father's wish that she learned to read and write." And here she would let out a deep sigh, and talk about her deceased husband at great length. The women of the chali already knew most of her tale. If anyone were to ask Ram Dui what happened when the big boss abused Sarita's father (he was a railway employee), Ram Dui would at once reply how it had enraged him to react by saying, "I'm not your servant but I'm a government servant. You can't threaten me in this manner. Look, if you humiliate me again, I'm going to break your jaw." What happened next? The big boss continued to insult Sarita's father, who in a fit of anger, punched the boss so hard on his neck that his hat flew off to the ground, and he almost passed out. But he was a robust man. He stepped forward and kicked Sarita's father in the stomach with his military boot rather hard. It ruptured his spleen, and he collapsed, dying without delay on the rail tracks. The government tried the man and Sarita's mother got five hundred rupees as compensation; but fate was not kind to them. Sarita's mother gave in to her urge to gamble. And so, within five months, she used up the money.

Sarita's mother did not tire of telling this story, but nobody knew if it was true or not. No one in the *chali* had any sympathy for Sarita's mother. Perhaps because they all deserved to receive sympathy from others. None had any friends. Most residents slept during the day and worked the night shift in the factory. Everyone lived close by, and yet they were distant, as no one had any interest in the other.

Almost everyone in the *chali* knew that Sarita's mother was forcing her daughter to be a prostitute, but since they did not bother about the happenings in the others' lives, they didn't care about contradicting Sarita's mother's words. "My daughter has little knowledge of this world!" she would say. However, once when Tukaram misbehaved with Sarita, one morning near the tap, she had screamed at Tukaram's wife. "Can't you control that bald husband of yours? May the Lord blind him with both eyes that cast evil eyes on my young girl! I swear, someday I'll thrash him so hard with my shoes that he'd have trouble existing. If he wants to be a rogue outside, that's all fine. But here he must behave like a gentleman."

When she heard it, Tukaram's squint-eyed wife came outside, tying the knots on her *dhoti*. "Be careful of what you say, you evil one!" she warned. "Your little goddess flirts with those hotel boys. Do you take us all to be blind fools? We know why every other day some new gentleman shows up at your door. And we know why your Sarita goes out often, all decked up! And you talk about respect and honor--- get lost from here!"

People around knew all about Tukaram's wife, especially about her affair with the kerosene seller. When he sold kerosene, she would call him inside her room and close the door. Sarita's mother did not forget to raise the point, and in a malicious voice said, "And your lover boy, that kerosene seller? For two long hours, he'd be inside your room. What did you do, sniff his kerosene?"

Despite such snide remarks, Sarita's mother wouldn't stay cross with Tukaram's wife for long. One day, Sarita's mother found Tukaram's wife whispering sweet nothings with a man in the dark night and the very next day Tukaram's wife also discovered Sarita, sitting with a 'gentleman' in a car. Later, both compromised and made friends again.

And so, Sarita's mother now asked Tukaram's wife, "Have you seen Sarita anywhere?"

Tukaram's squint-eyed wife glanced towards the narrow alley corner. "She's there, beside the garbage heap, playing with the village registrar's daughter." Keeping her voice low, she asked, "Kishori had just gone up. Did you meet him?"

Sarita's mother whispered, as her eyes scanned her surroundings. "I've just asked him to wait upstairs. But Sarita goes missing at the right moments. She understands nothing, she's only focused on playing for the whole day."

She proceeded towards the garbage heap, and when she reached the cemented urinal, Sarita stood up, her face stamped with a dejected expression. Her mother grabbed her arm roughly and said, "Come home, come! All you do is play around." While walking towards home, on the way, she slowly said, "Kishori is waiting for a long time. He's brought a rich gentleman with a car. Now you hurry, go upstairs, and get ready. Put on that blue georgette sari. Your hair is messy too. Get ready soon, then I'll comb your hair."

Sarita was excited to hear about the car with a gentleman. She was more interested in the car than in the man, as she loved car rides. When the car would speed through the open streets, and the wind whipped against her face, it filled her up with an unusual excitement. She felt then like a swan flying over the streets.

Sarita wasn't over fifteen years, but her behavior resembled more like thirteen-year-old girls. She disliked spending her time with women and engage in talks with them. She spent the best part of her day with smaller girls, playing silly games. For example, drawing white chalk lines on the dark asphalt of the alley interested her a lot. She drew the lines with such dedication that it seemed the world would perish if those chalk lines remained unetched. Or she would carry the jute sacks from their room and spend hours with her younger friends, cleaning the footpath, spreading them, and sitting on them, and such other foolish games.

Sarita was neither beautiful nor fair. Her face always

gleamed because of Bombay's humid climate. Her lips were thin and brown, as brown as the *chiku* (sapota) fruit, and they were always trembling. On her upper lip, below her nose, three or four beads of sweat always quivered and glistened.

She enjoyed good health. Despite living in a dirty environment, she had a rather neat and curvy body. It seemed the onslaught of youth had been quite a heavy one on her. Chubby and short, she looked healthier because of this. Rushing through the streets, when her skirt would billow up, passing men could see her calves, glistening like oiled teak, and devoid of any hair. The tiny pores on them reminded one of fresh orange, filled with sap, which with a little pressure would spray up to your eyes.

Her arms were round, and despite that she wore a rather ill-fitting blouse, her arms looked pretty. Her hair was long and thick, and smelled of coconut oil, and her thick braid, like a whip, patted her back. The length of her hair did not amuse her, as her braid interfered a lot when she played, and she did everything to keep it in place.

Sarita was quite oblivious to all worries. Two times a day, she would get her meal. Her mother managed the household chores. The only two tasks she did were to fill two buckets with water every morning, and every night, she got the lamp filled with oil spending a paisa. For years now she had been following this routine, and so each evening she would reach for the coins kept on the plate, and walk downstairs to buy oil for the lamp.

Sometimes- almost four or five times every month- when Kishori would bring the customers, she would be glad to accompany them to a hotel, or to some other dark locations. She ignored the other aspects of these nights, perhaps because she assumed some men like Kishori would also visit other girls' homes and they, too, had to go out with the gentlemen at night. And whatever happened with her, on those cold benches in Worli, or on the wet sand of Juhu, she imagined those to be happening with others, too. Once, she told her mother, "Ma, Shanta too is quite grown up now. You can send her with me too, right? The gentlemen order eggs for me, and Shanta is crazy about eggs." In an equivocal voice, her mother said, "Oh yes, I will send her with you once, after her mother returns from Pune."

Sarita, however, shared this good news with Shanta the very next day, as she returned from the open toilet. "When your mother returns from Pune, she shall resolve everything. You'd then come to Worli with me." And later, Sarita shared with her the night's incident that happened in the recent days. She spoke in a way that made it appear like a fairy tale. After listening to her story, Shanta, two years younger to Sarita, felt excitement quiver through her entire being. Sarita's words increased her appetite to hear more, and pulling her arm, she said, "Let's go downstairs, we'll talk there." And they went down, near the open toilet, where the shopkeeper Giridhari had spread out dirty pieces of coconuts to dry on jute sacks. There they stood for a long time, talking about exciting stories.

Sarita put on her blue georgette sari behind a makeshift curtain. The touch of cloth sent shivers through her body, and the very thought of the car ride filled her mind with a thrill. She wondered what the man would be like and where he would take her, hoping that the car ride should not be so short that they reach the hotel sooner than imagined. Then, inside the room, the man would start drinking and she'd feel suffocated to be there. She hated to be inside closed hotel rooms, where in the twin iron beds, she was not free to court sleep.

Soon, she draped the sari and smoothening out the creases, she stood before Kishori. "Kishori, have a look. Is the sari looking okay from behind?" Without waiting for her answer, she stepped towards the broken wooden box where she stored her Japanese rouge. She set a hazy mirror between the iron bars of the window. She bent a little and smeared powder on her cheeks. Then, she applied the rouge, and turned towards Kishori with a smile, seeking his approval.

Draped in the bright blue sari, her lips painted, and the onion-tinged rouge on her dusky cheek made her look like one of those toys that was sold the most during Diwali in the toy-sellers' shops.

Just then, Sarita's mother came in. With nimble hands, she combed Sarita's hair, and said, "Look my little girl, talk nicely, okay? And do whatever he says. This new man is very rich, he owns a car." Then, turning to Kishori, she said, "Now, you take her out. Poor man! He must be waiting for long!"

Outside, in the market, there was a factory wall that stretched long into the distance. A small board hung there that said, 'No Urinating here'. Inside a yellow car, three young men from Hyderabad were sitting, each one of them were holding a handkerchief over their noses. They would have taken the car further away, but the wall extended further down, along with the stench of urine.

The young man behind the steering wheel saw Kishori coming. He said to his friends, "Hey, he's here.... this is Kishori.... and ... this is..." His eyes were still on the car. "This girl looks very young. Do have a look, boys, the one in blue sari!"

When Kishori and Sarita approached the car, the two men in the backseat picked up their hats and made a space between them for Sarita to sit. Kishori opened the back door of the car and pushed Sarita inside with a prompt hand. He closed the door. The young man was sitting behind the driving wheel. Kishori said, "Sorry for being so late. She was visiting a friend, hence..."

The young man turned to look at Sarita. And then said to Kishori, "It's alright. But look..." Shifting over to the next seat, he leaned out of the window and asked, "She won't show tantrums, right?"

Kishori put his hand on his chest. "Trust me, Sir," he said.

The young man took out two rupees from his pocket and gave them to Kishori. "Have fun," he said.

As Kishori bowed, the car started.

It was five in the evening, and Bombay's roads were traffic choked. Cars, trams, buses, and people scurried everywhere. Quietly, Sarita sat crumpled up between two men. She scrunched her thighs together and rested her hands on her lap. Mustering a little courage, she spoke up, and then again stopped half-way. She felt like telling the driver to drive fast, as she felt rather suffocated sitting there.

There ensued silence in the car; the driver continued to drive. And the two men from Hyderabad, sitting in silence on the backseat, perhaps, thought about their proximity to a young girl, one who was theirs for a while, and with whom they could take some liberty without courting trouble.

The young man who drove the car had been living in Bombay for two years and had met many girls like Sarita during the day and night; in his yellow cab, various kinds of prostitutes had sat and therefore the matter didn't bother him much. His two friends had come from Hyderabad;

one among them was Shahab, who wanted to have an experience of the fast life of Bombay. So Kifayat, the young man who drove the car, planned with Kishori, and brought Sarita. Kifayat also wanted his second friend Anwar to have another girl. But Anwar declined, feeling it to be not right.

Kifayat had not seen Sarita before, because it was after a long time that Kishori brought a girl like her. Despite her charm, Kifayat's interest had not been in Sarita in particular. He could hardly pay attention to her as he was driving, too.

Sarita became very excited as the car moved towards the suburbs, leaving the city behind. The whiff of cool breeze and the speeding car elated her immensely, and she dropped her inhibition as a frenzy tore through her. She tapped her feet, swayed her arms, drummed her fingers, and her eyes chased the trees that rushed past the car.

Anwar and Shabab too relaxed. Shahab believed he could do whatever he wished with Sarita. Slowly, he put his hand around her waist. His touch tickled Sarita, and wiggling, she almost fell upon him, as her laughter spread out of the window. When Shahab tried to gain access to her waist for the second time, she doubled over, laughing out loud. Anwar stayed rooted to a corner.

Thrilled, Shahab said to Kifayat, "What a peppy girl she is!" He gave a tight pinch on Sarita's thigh. In return, Sarita twisted Anwar's ears, since he was sitting closer to her. Their laughter filled the car. It made Kifayat turn back, even though he could follow everything in the rearview mirror. In keeping with their hearty laughter, he sped the car.

Sarita wished she could sit on the hood of the car, almost next to the logo of the iron medallion of the flying angel. As she leaned forward, then Shahab poked her. To gain her balance, Sarita put her hands around Kifayat's neck. Kifayat kissed her hand. It sent a thrilling sensation through her body. Sarita jumped and went to the front seat, sitting next to Kifayat. Fondling his necktie, she asked, "What is your name?"

"My name?" he asked. "My name is Kifayat." Saying so, he handed her ten rupees note.

Sarita wasn't much interested in his name, but she took the note and pressed it inside her bra. Giggling like a child, she said, "You are an amiable man. And your necktie is nice too."

At that moment, everything appeared beautiful to Sarita. She wished that even the evil would turn good then, that the car kept speeding up, and everything collapsed into their heady moment. Her heart wished to sing. She stopped playing with Kifayat's necktie and hummed.

'It was you who taught me how to love/ it was you who woke my sleeping heart.'

After singing this film song for a while, she turned back, and looking at Anwar, she asked, "Why are you so quiet? Why don't you talk? Or, maybe sing a song?" Then, she jumped and came and sat on the backseat, and started combing Shahab's hair with her fingers. "Let's sing together. Do you remember the song *Devika Rani* (An Indian actress who acted in films in the period between 1930-1940. Known to be the first lady of Indian cinema) sang? *'I wish I could be a bird, singing in a forest'*- Devika Rani is so beautiful!"

She sang, and Shahab too gave his terrible voice to it.

And then, they started singing duets. Kifayat joined in by honking the horn with the rhythm of the song, and Sarita clapped her hands. Sarita's keen voice mingled with Shahab's gruffy one, merged with the honking horns, and created an orchestra. The winds rushed by, and the engine reverberated, adding to this.

Sarita, Shahab, Kifayat, they were all very happy. And watching them so cheerful, Anwar felt happy too, although he thought he was rather uptight with his inhibitions. His arms pricked with sensation, dormant desires stretched and spread within him, and he, too, was a part of their merry making.

While singing, Sarita took Anwar's hat from his head and put it on her head. She tried to see how it looked upon her, and hopped back to the next seat, to see her in the rearview mirror. Anwar wondered if he was wearing the hat from the beginning in the car.

Sarita slapped Kifayat's fat thigh and asked, "If I wear your trousers and shirt, with your tie, wouldn't I look like a complete businessman?"

Her talks were incomprehensible to Shahab, so he held and shook Anwar's arm, saying, "You're an idiot to give her that hat!" For a while, Anwar realized his foolishness.

Kifayat asked Sarita, "What's your name?"

"My name?" Sarita strapped the lace of the hat under her chin. "My name is Sarita."

Shahab remarked from the backseat, "Sarita, you're like a sparkler, not a mere woman!"

Anwar, too, wished to say something, but by that time Sarita was singing in a high-pitched voice. "I'm going to build a home in the town of love/ forsaking the rest of the world."

Kifayat and Shahab felt so happy that they wished the car kept ongoing for ever. Sarita continued to sing. The strands of hair came free from her plaits. They looked like dense smoke was spreading being lashed by air. She looked happy.

Shahab looked happy, Kifayat looked happy, and Anwar too made an effort to feel happy.

The songs ended, and they all felt, for a moment, that the pouring rains stopped abruptly.

Kifayat told Sarita, "Please sing another song."

Shahab rejoined from the back seat. "Yes, please, another one. The cinema people would find it too good."

Sarita sang. *"In my courtyard Ali has come/ I'm feeling dizzy with joy."*

The car moved with the rhythm of the song. Soon the road ended at the shore of the sea. The sun was about to set, and the cool breeze blew from the sea.

The car stopped. Sarita opened the door of the car, came out, and along the waves ran through the shore of the sea. Kifayat and Shahab also followed her. Under the tall palm trees, out in the open, so close to the sea and on the wet sand, Sarita did not know what was it she wanted- perhaps, she wished to merge with the Nature, dissolve in the sea, and be so tall that she could see those high palm trees from above! She wished her feet would absorb all the moisture... and everything would stay the same, the car, its speed, the breeze. She was over joyous. When the three young men from Hyderabad sipped beer, sitting on the wet sand of the beach, Sarita snatched the bottle away from Kifayat's hands and said, "Wait, I'll pour it for you."

Sarita poured the beer so fast that the foam came up to the edge of the glass. It pleased her. She dipped her fingers in the foam and licked her fingers. When the bitter taste bothered her, she made a long face. Kifayat and Shahab burst out laughing, and when Kifayat looked back, he saw that Anwar too was laughing.

The foam out of the six bottles of beer trickled through the wet sand; and the three of them consumed the rest. Sarita continued to sing. Once Anwar glanced at her, and he imagined her to be made of beer. On her dark cheeks, the cool breeze from the sea glistened. She felt elated, and so was Anwar. His heart wished for the sea water to turn into beer, and he would dive in with Sarita.

Picking up the two empty beer bottles, she clanged them together. It caused a reverberating sound, and Sarita burst out laughing. Kifayat, Shahab and Anwar also joined in.

Still laughing, Sarita said to Kifayat, "Let's drive the car now." Leaving the empty bottles on the wet sand, they ran and got inside the car. Strong breeze of air floated in, causing Sarita's long hair to fly in abandon.

They sang again.

The car tore through the air, like a saw. Sarita kept on singing. On the backseat, Sarita was sitting between Shahab and Anwar, who had already nodded off. Sarita ran her fingers through Shahab's hair, and he drifted off to sleep too. Shifting in the front seat, she sat next to Kifayat, and in a low voice said, "I've put your two friends to sleep. Now you too should sleep."

Kifayat smiled. "Then who's going to drive the car?"

Sarita smiled back. "It'll drive on its own."

For a long time, Kifayat and Sarita talked with each other. Soon, they reached the place where Kishori had brought Sarita to the car. When they reached near the wall that said, *"DO NOT URINATE HERE"*, Sarita said, "Please stop the car here."

The car stopped. Sarita got out, and waving him a goodbye, she started walking back home. His hands on the steering wheel, Kifayat was wondering about the entire incident, when Sarita stopped. Turning, she brought out the ten rupees note from inside her blouse, and kept it next to Kifayat, on the seat.

Surprised, Kifayat looked at the note. "Sarita, what is this?"

"Why should I take this money?" saying this, Sarita ran off, while Kifayat stared at the note in utter disbelief. When he turned back to look at his friends, he saw Shahab and Anwar were sleeping. Just like the ten rupee note on the seat.

Biographical Notes on Authors

Swarnakumari Devi

Born on August 28, 1855 Swarnakumari Devi was a Bengali poet, novelist, musician, and social activist who fought for women's liberation. Born into the illustrious Tagore family of Jorasanko, she was the elder sister of the Nobel laureate, Rabindranath Tagore. She was a versatile writer, one of the most outstanding Bengali women of the age, the first woman writer to gain prominence in her time. She wrote first in Bengali, later in English, and her works were quite popular during her lifetime. Her first novel Deepnirban (1870) was widely acclaimed. Among her other 25 works, *Chhinna Mukul, Snehalata and Kahake* are very famous.

Rabindranath Tagore

Born on May 7, 1861, Rabindranath Tagore was an Indian polymath- poet, novelist, composer, social reformer, and a painter. Mostly known for his poetry, 'the Bard of Bengal' wrote novels, essays, short stories, travelogues, dramas and well over thousands of songs. He was the first non-European to receive a Nobel prize in Literature for his much-acclaimed poem collection *Gitanjali* (1913). He was highly instrumental in introducing Indian culture to the West and he is regarded as the outstanding creative artist of early 20th-century. Other than Gitanjali, some of the most enduring works by him are *Gitabitan, Chokher Bali, Gora, Kabuliwala, Ghare-Baire* and others.

Sarat Chandra Chatterjee

Born on September 15 1876, Sarat Chandra Chatterjee was a Bengali novelist and short story writer of the early 20th century. Hailed as one of the greatest novelists in Indian literature, his works mirrored social injustices, superstitions, caste orthodoxy. In his hands, the novels became a powerful weapon of social and political reform. He is also considered to be a feminist who gave Indian literature some of its most powerful, iconic women characters. Some of his best-known novels are *Charitraheen, Pather Dabi, Devdas, Srikanta, Griha Daha, Sesh Prashna.*

Munshi Premchand

Born on 31 July 1880, Premchand (original name Dhanpat Rai Srivastav) was a pioneer of Hindi and Urdu social fiction. His first Hindi novel *'Sewa Sadan'* (1919) shot him to instant recognition. A novelist, short story writer, dramatist, and a translator, his works carried distinct social messages of the pre-independent India. The genre of short stories in India owes a lot to this great writer whose works focusses on social issues, plight of women, caste injustices, patriarchy, farmer's plight and many more. His notable works are *Godaan, Gaban, Mansarov*ar and others.

Rajsekhar Basu

Born on 16 March 1880, Rajsekhar Basu was a Bengali author mainly known for his humorous short stories. He wrote under the penname of *Parashuram*. His first book *'Gaddalika'* received praises from such personalities as Tagore. A creative writer par excellence, he was a chemist by profession and a man of several other achievements too. In 1958, Basu's collection of short stories, *'Anandibai Ityadi Galpa'*, won a Sahitya Akademi award for Bengali Literature. The Bengali dictionary completed by Rajsekhar is still widely used.

Jaishankar Prasad

Born on 30 January 1889, Jaishankar Prasad was a great Hindi poet, dramatist, and novelist. A celebrated personality related to Modern Hindi literature, he belonged to the Chhayawad or the Romatic era in Hindi literature. His first collection of poems *'Chitradhar'* was written in Braj dialect of Hindi. He was highly influenced by Sanskrit, Bengali, and Persian languages. *'Kamayani'* the most popular work penned by him, is indeed his magnus opus. His dramas, based on many great personalities of ancient India, proved to be the most pioneering ones in Hindi literature.

Bibhuti Bhushan Bandopadhyay

Born on 9 September 1894, Bibhuti Bhshan Bandopadhyay was a Bengali writer, who is best known for the autobiographical novel *Pather Panchali* (The song of the Road). His works are largely set in rural Bengal and in his works, he portrayed the challenges and realities of rural life. Like other writers of his time, his novels too examine the caste dynamics and the gradual decline of the rural economy in those first years after India attained independence. He was awarded the prestigious Rabindra Prize in 1951 for his beautiful novel *"Icchamati"*.

Saadat Hasan Manto

Born on 11 May 1912, Manto was an Indo-Pakistani writer, journalist, playwright who wrote mainly in Urdu. He produced 22 collections of short stories, a novel, several radio plays, essays, sketches, and these works established him as a non-conventional writer. Although he was charged with obscenity six times, his realistic portrayal of social issues, especially his stories about the partition of India, earned him wonderful accolades and established him as one of the finest Urdu writers of the 20th century.

Black Eagle Books

www.blackeaglebooks.org
info@blackeaglebooks.org

Black Eagle Books, an independent publisher, was founded
as a nonprofit organization in April, 2019. It is our mission
to connect and engage the Indian diaspora and the world at
large with the best of works of world literature published on a
collaborative platform, with special emphasis on
foregrounding Contemporary Classics and New Writing.

www.ingramcontent.com/pod-product-compliance
Lightning Source LLC
Chambersburg PA
CBHW050331110726
47899CB00007B/2455